A VILLA IN SICILY:

ORANGE GROVES AND VENGEANCE

(A Cats and Dogs Cozy Mystery—Book Five)

FIONA GRACE

Fiona Grace

Fiona Grace is author of the LACEY DOYLE COZY MYSTERY series, comprising nine books; of the TUSCAN VINEYARD COZY MYSTERY series, comprising seven books; of the DUBIOUS WITCH COZY MYSTERY series, comprising three books; of the BEACHFRONT BAKERY COZY MYSTERY series, comprising six books; and of the CATS AND DOGS COZY MYSTERY series, comprising nine books.

Fiona would love to hear from you, so please visit www.fionagraceauthor.com to receive free ebooks, hear the latest news, and stay in touch.

BOOKS BY FIONA GRACE

LACEY DOYLE COZY MYSTERY
MURDER IN THE MANOR (Book#1)
DEATH AND A DOG (Book #2)
CRIME IN THE CAFE (Book #3)
VEXED ON A VISIT (Book #4)
KILLED WITH A KISS (Book #5)
PERISHED BY A PAINTING (Book #6)
SILENCED BY A SPELL (Book #7)
FRAMED BY A FORGERY (Book #8)
CATASTROPHE IN A CLOISTER (Book #9)

TUSCAN VINEYARD COZY MYSTERY
AGED FOR MURDER (Book #1)
AGED FOR DEATH (Book #2)
AGED FOR MAYHEM (Book #3)
AGED FOR SEDUCTION (Book #4)
AGED FOR VENGEANCE (Book #5)
AGED FOR ACRIMONY (Book #6)
AGED FOR MALICE (Book #7)

DUBIOUS WITCH COZY MYSTERY
SKEPTIC IN SALEM: AN EPISODE OF MURDER (Book #1)
SKEPTIC IN SALEM: AN EPISODE OF CRIME (Book #2)
SKEPTIC IN SALEM: AN EPISODE OF DEATH (Book #3)

BEACHFRONT BAKERY COZY MYSTERY
BEACHFRONT BAKERY: A KILLER CUPCAKE (Book #1)
BEACHFRONT BAKERY: A MURDEROUS MACARON (Book #2)
BEACHFRONT BAKERY: A PERILOUS CAKE POP (Book #3)
BEACHFRONT BAKERY: A DEADLY DANISH (Book #4)
BEACHFRONT BAKERY: A TREACHEROUS TART (Book #5)
BEACHFRONT BAKERY: A CALAMITOUS COOKIE (Book #6)

CATS AND DOGS COZY MYSTERY
A VILLA IN SICILY: OLIVE OIL AND MURDER (Book #1)
A VILLA IN SICILY: FIGS AND A CADAVER (Book #2)
A VILLA IN SICILY: VINO AND DEATH (Book #3)

CHAPTER ONE

Audrey Smart dug her fingernails into the armrest as the tiny prop plane she was in touched down, bump-bump-bumping its way down the crude gravel runway in the midst of a watery haze. When she looked out the window, all she saw was barren landscape, stretching to black mountains in the distance that disappeared among the clouds.

Montagna.

She was finally here. And maybe, just maybe, so was her long-lost father.

That's why she'd come all this way, after all. To locate the father she'd idolized but hadn't seen since she was thirteen. The epic reunion of a lifetime, the stuff of Hallmark movies, with plenty of tears and tissues involved.

But it's not the only reason, a little voice inside her head screamed as she crawled to the front of the plane and the pilot helped her out onto the tarmac. The other three passengers—all locals, it seemed— were heading to a small white building that said, *Montagna Aeroporto,* so she followed along, dragging her overnight bag with her.

She really didn't want to think about the other reasons.

But the reasons—Reason Number One and Reason Number Two-- seemed to *want* to be thought about. Every time they'd threatened to swarm her head during the half-hour flight, she'd thumped the side of her head, nudging them out. It hadn't helped.

When she turned her phone off airplane mode, she saw a text from Reason Number One: *Hope you're having a good time. Miss you.*

She growled a little under her breath. Mason Legare, her hot expat neighbor who lived a block away from her home in Mussomeli, Sicily, where she ran her veterinarian practice, was handsome, sweet, helpful, and . . . had the *worst* possible timing.

When she reached the shade of the airport, she hesitated and considered responding. In the end, she didn't. It was Mason who'd forced her out here, on what was probably a wild goose chase, before she'd really researched it fully. Mason and . . .

Her phone buzzed. A text from G, owner of *La Mela Verde,* the most popular café in Mussomeli. *Looking forward to our date, Principessa.*

"Ugh," she said aloud, wanting to wring both their necks. The last thing she wanted to think about was going on a date. The word "date" had actually made her break out in a case of hives.

And yet, she had two coming up this weekend, one with Mason, and one with G. The two of them, with their terrible timing. Terrible timing was the story of her life. After beating around the bush from the second she arrived in Mussomeli, over four months ago, they'd each finally confessed they wanted to date her . . . for real.

To say it'd made her head spin was an understatement. And she liked both of them, for entirely different reasons, so she couldn't say no. For a while there, she'd thought it was Mason, the American who understood all her challenges living in a foreign country. But then, when she saw G, she couldn't deny that she liked him, too. He was the welcoming face she'd first met in Mussomeli, and one of the main reasons why she was happy to call the place home. He'd made her feel so welcome and had always been there for her with a nice bowl of *ciambotta* and some friendly conversation.

It was enough to drive her insane.

The only thing she could think was to escape, even though she'd just arrived back in town after a stint cleaning up a stray cat problem in Lipari, an island off the northern coast of Sicily.

Luckily, she'd had Concetta, her assistant, who, after learning of her "man problems," suggested she take a day off to mull it over and decide what to do. She'd seen the big welts popping out on Audrey's skin and ordered her to take a rest to clear her mind.

Man problems? Since when had Audrey ever, in her thirty-five years, had man problems? The biggest problem she'd ever had was with them staying far *away* from her.

And now that she had *two* men, she also had hives.

But when she'd thought about escape, the first thing she'd thought about, of course, was the source of her First Man problems, the one from which all of her problems seemed to somehow stem from . . .Montagna. Her father.

Audrey almost laughed about it as she made her way to the curb and stepped into a smelly taxi, the only one at the curb. She looked at the notes she'd scribbled, an address of a man named Smart, the only one in the Montagna phone directory. Instead of speaking in her fractured Italian, she showed the driver the crumpled paper. He nodded, and they were off.

The town of Montagna, in Northern Italy, was even more remote than the island of Lipari. Lipari had its share of tourists, but this place was completely off the map. When they left the airport behind them, they drove through a town consisting only of dirt roads. As it puffed up around them in a thick, choking haze, Audrey squinted to see the sights. Children playing barefoot in the street. A woman in what looked like a pioneer dress and headscarf, carrying a basket full of laundry. Houses that were barely more than one-room shacks, slapped together with random pieces of discarded wood.

Sure, Dad. I can see the allure of this place. You left us for THIS?

Growing up, Audrey's father had been her favorite person on Earth. Everything she'd done so far to fix up the one-dollar house she'd bought in Sicily, she'd learned from him. Though she remembered little of their time together, since it was so long ago, those lessons had stayed with her. Those lessons, and the memory of a postcard he used to keep in his breast pocket.

A picture of this place, *Montagna.*

She wrinkled her nose as she remembered the old photograph. It had been beautiful. Peaceful. Restful, the picture of the sun setting over the black mountains as the sunset dissolved into the sea. Two seagulls danced in the pink-orange skies. It hadn't looked like *this*. Had it?

Of course, it *might* have. The picture had been taken just during sunset. The darkness could've hidden a wealth of problems.

More power to you, Dad, but if I'd dreamed all my life of this place and arrived here, she thought as she watched a child in a too-small shirt that bared his belly, wheeling an old, bald tire down the street, *I'd probably be on the next flight out.*

But even though she'd last seen him over twenty years ago, she'd never forgotten that postcard. Never given up hope that one day, she'd reunite with him. And now, he was so close. So when Concetta told her she should take a day off to decompress, she decided to grab it. She already had the ticket. Now, it was time to satisfy her burning curiosity, once and for all.

Who knew? Maybe her father would invite her in, be so happy to see her, make her a big bowl of pasta, and insist she stay with him for the next week? She could just see her calling both of her beaus, saying, *something came up,* and cancelling both dates. Maybe for good. Right now, she didn't want to think about letting either of them down. She couldn't.

But she had to go back. Her clinic was waiting for her.

Tonight. She'd go back and make her decision about which date to keep, tonight.

Right now, it was time to meet her father.

The taxi pulled onto a road of sand, by the beach. Here, there were little bungalows with thatched roofs, just steps from the sea. Though they were nothing more than hovels, one couldn't beat the view of the aqua Tyrrhenian Sea, speckled with small, green islands. Men and women sat on the front steps to their houses, watching her carefully, as the taxi went by. Children picked through the sand, their laughter ringing out in the warm air. A fisherman who was about to cast out a line turned to eye her, too. Audrey got the feeling they didn't get much traffic around here.

Well, if my father wanted peace and quiet from the hustle and bustle of Back Bay Boston, this sounds like the place to go.

The taxi pulled up at a small blue home that was choked by seagrass. Of all the homes, it was the prettiest and least rundown, except for perhaps the house next to it. Some of the others looked like Three Little Pig homes, constructed of slapped-together materials that might blow over in a stiff breeze. This house, though, while small, looked like it had been constructed by a master carpenter. Just like . . .

Dad?

A garden of wildflowers was dotted with broken seashells, full of sand. Olive trees hung low over the path to the door, creating a canopy. Audrey stared at it, hand on the taxi's door handle, unable to move.

The driver cleared his throat. *"Sedici al mare,"* he said, pointing to the slip of paper she'd given him. He also motioned to the door, as if to say, *Go on.*

"Oh. This is it?"

He nodded.

"Grazie mille," she said, handing him the fare.

She stepped outside and shivered despite the near eighty-degree temperature. The cab sped off the second she closed the door, effectively quashing any hopes she had of retreat. Pushing aside tree branches, she peered into the open windows, hoping to get a glimpse of the home's inhabitants, but the inside was dark. She concentrated on

4

putting one foot in front of the other, worried that they'd fail her or send her running away, after the cab.

He'd been gone from her life over twenty years. Twenty years, he could've come back. And yet he'd never even written, never told her where he was going. He hadn't even said goodbye, and her mother had refused to speak of him, as if his mere name was a dirty word. Whenever Audrey asked her mother if she still had contact with him, the answer was always the same, "It doesn't matter. He's out of our life for good, and good riddance."

She should've been angry, but she wasn't . . . just curious. She'd made her way in life without him, without his help. She wanted nothing from him. She just wanted to know the man who'd given her life. She didn't care if he'd be unhappy to see her, or if he sent her away . . . she just wanted to know who he was, now. And, most importantly, *why* he'd gone.

That wasn't too much to ask, was it?

Squaring her shoulders, she quickly took the last few steps and stood in front of the battered screen door. Not finding a doorbell, she rapped on the frame. "Hello?"

There was movement inside that, at first, she attributed to the breeze, blowing things inside the house. But then she noticed a tall, substantial silhouette rising from deeper in the house, slowly making its way toward her.

Her breath hitched.

The features slowly came into view. So much was different, but as the characteristics materialized in front of her, yes, she could see the resemblance to the man she once knew. A strong chin, now gray and grizzled. A once slightly balding head, now with just a few renegade wisps of hair reaching for the sky. Perpetually tanned skin from framing homes outdoors, now leathered from the sun. Eyes that were deep blue and somewhat sad, as if filled with regret. Regret for leaving one's family?

He stopped, fingers on the door handle, a question on his face.

She swallowed. "Dad?"

CHAPTER TWO

The curiosity on the man's face turned to something like horror. The eyes narrowed to slits. The wrinkles on his weathered face grew more pronounced. He gritted his teeth for a long moment, before erupting in a string of Italian that didn't seem to have an end.

It was in that long moment that Audrey realized a few things. Her father had had a tattoo on his forearm of a four-leaf clover. He'd had a Roman nose, not the flat, broad nose of this man. And this man had a purplish birthmark on his cheek.

So . . . not her father. Had she really been that blind?

No . . . no, somehow, she knew she wouldn't meet her father, here. But somewhere, deep inside, she'd harbored a childish hope. The hope of a twelve-year-old girl who'd lost her hero, forever.

She took a step backwards. "Um, I'm sorry. Do you speak English? *Lei parla inglese?* I'm looking for my father. Do you know a Miles Smart?"

His eyes narrowed. "Smart?"

She felt anything but smart, at that moment. "Yes. I thought there was someone by that name living here?" She fumbled for her phone. Maybe she could bring it up and show him. "At least, in the records I looked up online, it said--"

He shook his head. "No. No Smart."

Audrey's spirits plummeted. *Well, so much for that.*

"Oh. *Grazie.* I'm sorry to bother you," she said, stepping away. She turned around and realized she had no ride back to the airport. In fact, the next flight wouldn't leave until later that afternoon, according to the schedule she'd taken from the Messina airport, which offered flights to the several small towns on the mainland for a dear price. She reached for her phone and gazed at the display. No service.

Well, the airport wasn't that far away. I could probably walk it.

She took a step and heard a loud bang, somewhere nearby. For a moment, she thought it had to be a car backfiring. That's what it had to be, right? This wasn't America, after all. It couldn't be a gunshot, right? Not in this idyllic little town in Italy that her father had longed to live in.

But then, a couple of slouchy-looking teenagers went running down the street like a bolt of lightning, looking over their shoulders, as if they knew someone would be in pursuit. One of them was clutching something black . . . which *definitely* could've been a gun.

Eyes wide, she turned to go back to the house, hoping she could ask to use the phone. If they even had phone lines around here. Or for shelter, in case those teens caught sight of her and decided to mug her. She clutched her bag to her chest, wishing she hadn't brought so many euros with her. Back then, her thought process had been: *What if I love the place as much as my dad and want to by a souvenir t-shirt? Or stay in a hotel for a night? Or . . .*

Dumb, dumb, dumb. All of it. She didn't want to stay another *second* in this place.

Maybe her father had felt the same way.

That was when a woman stuck her head out from the nice bungalow next door. She waved slightly. "You're looking for Miles Smart?" she said in an accent that sounded vaguely Australian.

She nodded, excited. "Yes. That's right. Have you heard of him?"

The pretty woman nodded. "He's not here anymore. Hasn't been here for at least ten years. Are you his daughter?"

"Yes."

She smiled. "I can tell. You have his smile."

"You actually met him?" Audrey asked, looking at her. She was older, old enough to be Audrey's mother. Of course, her father and this woman would've gotten along. He'd probably helped her with her repairs, which was why her house was nicer than most on the street. Maybe they were even lovers. Audrey had been young when her parents had separated, but her memories of her parents' marriage were rocky ones, full of loud arguments that seemed to last long into the night. But her mother never spoke of him at all. She didn't even know if they'd gotten a divorce.

Of course, she knew her father had moved on. But somehow, seeing this woman, the woman he'd moved on *to*, faded her excitement over finding someone who actually knew him.

"I used to call him Smile Smart," she said with a girlish giggle, much to Audrey's annoyance. But the woman was so caught in a memory of her father, she didn't seem to notice. "He had the nicest smile. I'm Dinah."

Audrey wasn't in the mood for introductions to the woman who'd spent time with her father that was supposed to be *hers*. She opened her mouth to say more when Dinah added, "Audrey, right? Or are you Sabrina? He spoke about you often. You look like Audrey. He showed me your picture."

He had? She had a burning desire to know exactly what he'd said, but instead, she asked, "Do you know where he went?"

She laughed. "He moved on. Your father didn't strike me as the type of person who wanted to put down roots. One day, he just up and left. Didn't even say goodbye."

Audrey let out a sigh. *That sounds familiar.* "You never heard from him again?"

"Oh, no. I did. I get postcards, now and then. Very rarely. The last one I got was about a year ago. Maybe two." She pushed away from the window, found something out of view, and held it out to Audrey. "I kept it on my icebox because it was so pretty. Here. You can have it."

She took it and looked at the photograph. It was of another beach, somewhere, with white sands and a castle in the distance. She turned it over. The postmark was smudged, just a jumble of letters, so she couldn't tell where it'd been sent from. Of course. Underneath was a sweeping script she didn't recognize.

Hello, Dinah, love! And greetings from my new corner of the world. Don't think I'll be here long; too much wind! But the sea is deep blue, just the shade of your eyes. So every time I look out the window, I think of you. And I hope one day to see you again. All my love, MILES

Audrey stared at it, her stomach sinking. He'd loved other women, since Audrey, her mom, and her sister. And now he was gone, possibly off to love even more other women. Maybe he had dozens of them, in towns all over the world.

She turned it over and gazed at the picture, trying to determine where it was from. The postcard was a clue, and yet how was it possible to say so much and give away so little? It was almost as if Miles Smart didn't *want* to be found.

And maybe that was the point.

Maybe, she should just let sleeping dogs lie.

"He likes to travel," she mused.

"Always. A tumbleweed. That's what your father always called himself."

Audrey pointed to the picture. "Where is this? Do you know?"

Dinah shrugged. "No clue. I think it might be the French Riviera, but I'm not much of a vagabond myself. He asked me to go along with him, but I was too happy, right here. But he did love the beach. He said he was going west." She looked as if there was something she wanted to say, paused, and then said, "I should let you know . . . your father told me that with you, and your sister? He stayed as long as he could. Fifteen years. He said it was a record for him. He really wanted to raise you, but he kept feeling that pull. He couldn't resist it. He wanted to be there."

But he wasn't. Not when I needed him most. Which might have been worse than if he was never there at all.

She sighed and said, "Thank you for the information, may I keep this?"

Dinah nodded. "Of course."

"Also, may I use your phone, if you have one? I have a flight to catch."

The woman nodded and opened the door for her. She thanked her and went inside, already exhausted at the thought of travelling back, so soon after she'd gotten here. But this was a dead end. She had to resolve in her heart that there was a good chance her father would never be found.

*

Audrey's cab finally pulled into Mussomeli at a little after six o'clock. She had the driver stop at her clinic. The second she stepped onto the curb, she saw her pet fox, Nick, waiting for her. It was the nicest thing she'd seen, after an altogether disappointing day.

"Hey, Bub!" she said as the animal wrapped itself around her calves like a cat, excitedly wanting a pet. "I missed you, too. One second. Let me see what's up at the clinic and then we'll be on our way home. Want an apple?"

She lifted him up and he licked her face. She laughed, then went inside, yawning. *There is nothing like a warm-and-furry to make all your worries melt away.*

Concetta was just opening the door to let the last appointment of the day out. She looked tired, like it'd been a hard few hours. "Hi, Concetta!" Audrey said as she dropped her bag on the floor. "Hard day?"

The model-pretty girl with the long light hair yawned. She was a veterinary student in Palermo, trying to get her clinical hours so that she could become a full-fledged veterinarian, and had been, over the past few weeks, Audrey's lifesaver. "Just long. Appointments, morning to night. But routine."

"Any problems?"

She shook her head. "What about you? Did you find your father?"

"No. Seems like he was there, years ago, but he left." She pulled out the postcard and waved it. "So I have another clue. Not that it's much of a clue."

Concetta took the postcard and read it. "Where is this?"

"No idea. It doesn't look familiar to you?"

"No, it is not much to go on, is it? That's sad."

"I suppose it might be the Universe's way of telling me I should give up and forget about it. After all, my dad's probably forgotten about me. So maybe there's no point." *Even though Dinah said he mentioned me often. If he did, why did he never send ME a postcard? He'd spent fifteen years with my family but wiped his hands of us. Why did he completely cut me out of his life?*

She waved those thoughts away. She'd spent the entire flight back, thinking about it. Unfortunately, the mission had been a failure. She'd set out, hoping to answer questions, but instead, she found herself with more confusion, a bigger mystery to solve. And she definitely didn't need that right now. Not when . . .

"So did you decide which of your two hunks you're going to date this weekend? You have your first one tonight, right? With G?"

Audrey winced at the question. She hadn't decided squat.

"I don't know what to do! Tell me." When Concetta just shrugged, she said, "This is terrible. I'm no closer to making a decision than I was when I left."

"Well, you could always—"

"I know. I'll flip a coin." She rifled through her bag and pulled out a quarter she'd been holding onto since she left America. "Heads, I'll go out with Mason. Tails, I'll go out with G."

10

She flipped it into the air, meaning to catch it, but she missed it when she tried to snatch it from the air. It skidded across the tile and landed underneath one of the waiting room chairs. She rushed to it and stooped. "Heads."

"What does that mean, again?" Concetta asked.

"It's . . . I think it meant I was going to go out with Mason. Or was I going to send regrets to Mason? Ugh!" She threw up her hands. "I can't remember."

She fell back on her butt and ran her hands down her face. "I'm going to go crazy."

"Well, what I was going to say, Audrey, is that you haven't committed to either of them, have you?"

Audrey looked at her, eyes bleary. "No. Of course not."

"So, you're allowed to date both of them. That's what dating is, isn't it? To see if you like a man? Like, you try, see if you like? No one said you had to be exclusive."

"But . . . they don't know about each other. So isn't that kind of like . . . cheating?"

"Cheating?" Concetta laughed. "How can you be cheating if you're not committed?"

Not committed. Audrey mulled that over. She hadn't made any promises to anyone . . .

Suddenly, it was as if a light bulb clicked on in Audrey's head. What the young girl said was absolutely true. And it was exactly what her older sister Brina would've told her, had she been here—Brina had dated a new guy, practically every day, in college, until she met her husband. "You know, you're right. I never thought about it like that, but that makes sense."

She nodded. Though she was probably ten years Audrey's junior, she'd probably had a lot more man-experience than Audrey did. Audrey's love life in Boston had been pining after men who wanted her for nothing more than a tumble in the coat closet.

Right now, as Audrey stared at Concetta, the answer seemed so simple. So obvious.

"Then I'll do that. And I don't have to let anyone down . . . yet. That'll be okay, right?"

"Right!"

She checked the time on her phone. It was just after six, which gave her a couple hours to get ready. G had told her that they'd go out for a

11

late dinner at a bistro by his house, at around eight, eight-thirty. Sicilians were pretty flexible on times. As a resident of the town since birth, he knew Mussomeli and all of its inhabitants, and they all loved him. He spread light and cheer wherever he went, not to mention he was an amazing cook. Not to mention, he was strong and handsome, a little bit of a bad-boy, with his dark Italian looks and tattoo sleeves up each arm. She definitely could do worse than having G as a boyfriend.

"All right. I'd better get home and—"

Just then, the door opened, and a woman stepped in with a small teacup poodle, cradled in her arms. Worriedly, she started to speak in Italian, her words coming in such a staccato, rapid-fire way that Audrey couldn't translate a single one of them. She looked to Concetta.

Concetta said, "She said Bambino, here, ate a small pinecone today. She thought he coughed it up and would be fine, but he's been acting strange, all day."

One look at the dog confirmed that Bambino wasn't quite right. His head was lolling on his owner's arm, and he looked miserable. "Has he had diarrhea? Vomiting?"

The woman continued to gesticulate as she spoke. Concetta gasped. "She said he had a seizure!"

Audrey sprung to action. "Hand him to me," she said, gathering him into her arms. "He's going into anaphylaxis due to the sap in the pinecone. We'll need to inject him at once and get him on an IV."

The women rushed into the surgery room, where Audrey instructed Concetta where to find the epinephrine. Once she had it, Audrey told Concetta, "Get the IV started."

Audrey administered the life-saving medicine. Concetta started the IV, and the animal was too tired to protest to any of their work. This was the sign of a very sick animal.

Once she was finished, she went out to the front and said to the owner, "Yes, he's very sick. But it's a good thing you brought him in when you did. We'll keep him here tonight for observation, of course, but I think your Bambino will be just fine in the morning."

Concetta translated, and the woman clutched at her heart. "*Grazie! Grazie mille!*"

She hugged Audrey and Concetta with relief, then went in to pet Bambino and kiss his cheek. Audrey smiled as she watched the obvious concern in the pet owner's eyes. It was a nice thing to see, and even nicer to be able to help little animals and their owners in this way. That was why she'd never get tired of this job. The look of gratefulness in their eyes almost made up for her terrible day.

Concetta walked the pet owner to the door, telling her that all would be okay as she gently rubbed her back. When the woman left, Audrey clapped her hands.

"Well, I guess that settles it. I can't go on my date tonight. I have to stay here with Bambino."

Concetta shook her head and pointed for the door. "Go. I'll stay here. There's nothing you can do anyway that I can't do. That is an order!"

"But—"

"I have absolutely nothing to do, tonight! So stop making excuses," Concetta said with a laugh. "You'd better hurry or you'll be late for your date!"

"All right, all right, I'm going!" she said as the younger woman walked her to the door. She scooped up her bag and turned. "Just t—"

"Text you if I need anything. I know, I know," she said, holding the door open. "Have fun on your date!"

I don't know about that, Audrey thought as she headed out. *But I'll try.*

CHAPTER THREE

Audrey was deep in thought as she walked down one of Mussomeli's narrow, cobblestone streets, toward her home, *Piazza Tre*. She nearly tripped over Nick three times, and waved absently at the owner of *il Mercado del Pepe*, who was pulling in the sidewalk bins of vegetables. As he often did, he gave her a paper bag filled with the ripest tomatoes and peppers and apples he hadn't been able to sell.

She hardly realized what was happening until she'd taken a few steps with the bag in her hand. She whirled. *"Scusi,"* she said. "I mean, *Grazie. Buona sera, Luigi."*

He tipped an imaginary hat to her. "Have you heard the latest news, *cara?"*

She stopped. It was a small town, and yet the people here seemed to love their gossip. Last week, while she'd been in Lipari, one of the town boys had gone to the mainland to race sportscars. Before that, the main piazza had been filled with smoke because Mama Rivalta had left her pasta sauce cooking when she went to church, and it'd blown the lid of her pressure cooker so hard and so high that it'd embedded itself in the plaster of her ceiling. The photographs had been on the front page of Mussomeli's local newspaper. "No. What is it now?"

"There are new owners in the Tivoli estate."

Audrey frowned. "The Tivoli estate? Where is that?"

Just then, his wife, Carmen, came out. "Tivoli. You see. Oranges?" She pointed vaguely.

"Oh!" Audrey understood, now. She'd definitely seen the estate, because it was perfectly visible from the large picture window in her bedroom. A sprawling hillside with rows and rows of pretty orange trees, and beyond that a gorgeous white mansion with a burnt sienna tiled roof, baking under the sun. It had one of those courtyards, the walls climbing with vines, that reminded Audrey of a Spanish mission. But as beautiful as it was, there was nothing more wonderful than the smell of citrus that greeted her, every time she threw open her shutters. "Oh, I know it. What about it? It was for sale, right? Probably for more than a dollar, huh?"

With my luck, the new owners will probably knock it down and put a shopping mall there. Just what I need, to escape America to live in view of another shopping mall.

"*Si.* The owners—not so good." His thick gray brows knitted into one.

"Not so good? What does that mean?" she asked, now genuinely curious.

He leaned in closer. "The Piccolo clan used to live there. And I think there are more of them in there, now. The clan is one of the meanest and worst. Cosa Nostra," he whispered.

"Cosa . . ." She gasped. "Wait. You mean mafia?"

He nodded and pressed a finger to his lips. "Shh. But yes."

She looked around. The street was empty. What did he think—they were spying on him with satellites from outer space? She knew the mafia were good and had eyes everywhere, but they weren't *that* good. Were they? "Have you seen them?"

"No. No one has. The "for sale sign" come down, though. They do everything the same—in the middle of the night. No witnesses."

That sounded shady. She blinked, wondering if she could see them and all their illegal goings-on from her bedroom window. Would that make her a witness? A wanted woman? She'd seen a Lifetime movie about that, once.

Knowing my luck, probably, and they'll make a Lifetime movie about me, too.

"A good girl like you must stay away from them. You hear me? They are not good to get tied up with."

"Oh. Great. I'll keep that in mind." She sighed. Unless they had pets, she probably wouldn't see them at all, considering how much she worked at the clinic. "Have a good night, Luigi."

She was vaguely aware that he was watching her curiously as she made her way toward her home. "You be careful! You have much on your mind, *Dottore.*"

She nodded. *Tell me about it.*

She didn't want to add mafia to the list. Though she'd agreed with Concetta that dating two different men in the same weekend wasn't a problem because neither was a proposal of marriage, she still felt, well . . . dirty about it. Part of it was because though G and Mason knew each other, they didn't exactly like each other. And no matter which way she sliced it, neither would be happy to know she was spending time with

15

the other one. She wouldn't tell them, of course, but what if they found out? They'd be upset. So it felt like a betrayal.

Not to mention, the thing with her dad. That had been a big bust. And finding out that he was a wanderer, who didn't stay in one place for long . . . it just seemed that she'd never find him.

Why couldn't anything in her life be easy?

But it was too late to cancel on the men. She'd go on one date with each of them—just one—and make her decision from there.

With that thought solidified in her head, she walked the rest of the way home, feeling slightly better to have made a plan.

When she got to her house at *Piazza Tre,* her quaint little house on the corner, the camera crews were out again, taking panoramic shots of the street. She groaned. They were *always* taking panoramic shots of the street; the road and its residents were destined to be better known than the residents of Sesame Street, once her neighbor Nessa got done with it. Nessa was a California girl who'd also gotten a one-dollar house, and was now filming her own HGTV show, a tidbit she seemed to work in to almost every conversation she had.

Audrey quickly rushed to her door, keeping her head down so she could avoid the camera and a possible run-in with her witchy neighbor. Luckily, she managed to get inside and close the door.

She flipped on a light and looked around the kitchen. Ah. It wasn't quite home yet, but it was getting there. She'd done this room up nice, and so just walking in, smiling at the lemon décor she'd put everywhere, made her smile. It even *smelled* like lemons. She inhaled deeply. Every time she walked through the arched doorway, a little voice inside her repeated, *Mine. This is all mine.*

Nick whined. She grabbed an apple from the bag and went to wash it. As she did, she noticed the base of the faucet was wet.

Oh, god. Is that a leak?

She opened the doors under the sink. Sure enough, the bottom of the cabinet was wet.

"Great," she muttered, grabbing a bucket and shoving it underneath. As she did, water dripped on her hand.

Mine. All mine, the voice said, but this time, it was a rueful whine.

She'd been so proud when she'd installed the antique bronze fixture, since plumbing had never been her dad's thing. He'd always contracted out for that stuff. It looked perfect, really bringing out the rustic touches of the kitchen. She'd been so proud of the kitchen, period, because it'd been the first room in her one-dollar house that she'd redone, entirely on her own. Well, with a little help from Mason. There was plenty more to do, but this felt like a step back. *Of course, I screwed it up. This is something Mason would know how to fix in a jiffy.*

She cringed. No way was she asking him for help, considering she was dating his rival, in, oh, forty minutes and counting.

Which reminds me, I have to get ready.

Audrey cut Nick the apple and set it in his dish. Then she grabbed a wrench and set to work, trying to tighten everything that needed tightening. She couldn't seem to find anything that wasn't done perfectly according to the YouTube video she'd watched. The more she went along, the more exasperated she became, until she was hurling curses into the air like a sailor.

"This is all new! New fixtures! New washers! New copper!" She growled as water continued to drip in her face. "How can this be happening?"

When she pulled out from under the sink to find another washer, she happened to look up at the clock on the wall.

It read 8:15.

"Holy—" she shouted, sitting up so fast that she banged her forehead against the inside of the cabinet frame. "OW!"

Dizzy and clutching her throbbing head, she rushed upstairs, grabbed her robe, and flew into the shower off the kitchen. She took a thirty-second, world-record-breaking shower, then hurled herself upstairs and threw on a nice sundress. Breathing hard, she slathered on a little lip gloss and gazed at herself in the mirror. "Not too terrible for ten minutes," she said, staring at herself. "Not—"

Her eyes caught on the purple welt on her forehead. The pain hadn't subsided much, and the bruise was getting angrier and angrier with each passing second, adding more colors. Now, it seemed to have a bit of red in there, as well. A practical sunset of pain.

She rummaged in her make-up kit for her concealer and dabbed it on the painful bruise. It didn't help. "Forget it," she muttered, tossing it down in disgust.

As she did, her eyes caught on the picture window across from her. She went to it and stared out the window, at the orange groves, arranged in neat little lines. She inhaled the scent of the oranges and tried to spy some sign of movement in the mansion. But there was none.

She thought of what Luigi had said to her and shuddered: *They do everything the same—in the middle of the night. No witnesses.*

Audrey squinted and stared into all the house windows, but the shades in each one were drawn tight.

Mafia. In there?

She'd believe it when she saw it.

*

At eight-thirty, someone rapped lightly on her door.

Her date. Date number one.

"Buona sera, Principessa!" G said brightly as she opened the door. He was rather dressed up, by G standards, in light khakis and loose linen shirt, as opposed to his normal work uniform of jeans and t-shirt. Handsome, definitely.

And he held out to her a lovely red rose.

"Hello," she said with a smile, her nerves still zinging. "Oh, for me?"

He laughed. *Smart, Audrey. Who else would it be for?*

Blushing, she took the rose, popped in a glass of water in her kitchen, and stepped outside, pulling her wrap tight around her. When she arrived at the front stoop, G was kneeling down, greeting Nick, giving him a playful head rub.

The second he looked up at her, he visibly recoiled. "Oh, poor thing. What happened to your lovely head?"

She touched the painful welt gently. "Nothing. Just a casualty of war."

"You mean, fixing the house?"

"Yep."

"You know, you can always ask me for help! I would be happy to lend my hands to you!"

She hadn't ever asked him, mostly because he was known for his food, not his handyman skills. That was Mason. And Mason had always been able and willing to help. She probably could've used both of their help, honestly, considering how much work there was to be done. But the thought of the fireworks that would happen if the two crossed paths made her cringe.

"Thanks." She couldn't help looking up and down the street, expecting, with her luck, to see Mason rounding the corner. He only lived a couple of blocks away, after all. She shivered. "Where are we off to?" she asked, wanting to get there as soon as possible to avoid such a possibility.

"A little place I know at the edge of town. A bistro you will like, with a dance floor. You like dancing?"

"Well . . . I don't actually know how to dance very well," she admitted as they walked in the direction of the main piazza, which was, thankfully, in the opposite direction of Mason's house. Other than a couple of lessons from her dad where she'd stand on her father's toes as he waltzed her around, she hadn't really had the opportunity or the desire. "You do?"

He nodded. "I love to dance. That's all right, I will teach you."

She let out a shuddering breath. She didn't want to be a party pooper, but dancing was the last thing she wanted to do after such an exhausting day. *He's losing points for this, and Mason's gaining them.* She could never see Mason, tripping the light fantastic in those big cowboy boots of his. "I'm a little tired. It was a crazy day. Maybe we can just take it easy and—"

"Of course," he said as he put an arm around her, squeezing her close on the narrow street to avoid an oncoming car. "You had a trip, yes? Where did you say you were off to?"

"Montagna, Italy," she said as they rounded the corner to a section of town she'd never been to. There was a storefront for an actual cobbler there; little hand made shoes for children and adults, lined up in the front display. It was little unexpected, old-world things like this that made her love Mussomeli. "Have you heard of it?"

He nodded, brow creasing. "Not much up there. And from what I hear, some bad people there. Not very safe for a young woman, travelling alone. What brought you there?"

She swallowed. She'd told Mason a little about her father leaving, and he'd understood. G probably would, too, but it felt like too much of a sob story. And this was supposed to be fun. A date. She said, "Oh. Just had a ticket and wanted to check it out."

"You were not gone long. Just the day?"

"Yes. And I don't think I'll be back," she said with a shrug. "To tell you the truth, after Lipari and Montagna, I'm happy to stay in

19

Mussomeli and spread my roots a little bit more. Too much excitement, ping-ponging all over the place. I'm tired."

He laughed. "Well, then, a nice, relaxing meal is in order!"

"That sounds perfect," she said with relief.

CHAPTER FOUR

The place G selected was at an outdoor terrace, sparkling with fairy lights, with sweeping views of the countryside. A band consisting of a flute and tambourine was playing lively folk music as a number of men and women danced a flirtatious tarantella, long red skirts swishing as they clapped in unison. Audrey watched them effortlessly perform the steps. *G wanted me to do that? I'd wind up dancing off the terrace to my death, probably.*

As they reached the front gate, she looked over to see Nick, begging hopefully for admittance. "No, Bub. You can't go in there. But I'll bring you a doggie bag. Okay?"

He seemed to pout for only a second before letting out a sharp howl and disappearing down an aisle.

G knew the host, which was no surprise. After laughing and joking in Italian, the host led them to what must've been the best table in the house, at the edge of the terrace, overlooking the valley. She wasn't prone to vertigo, but in the dying sunlight, Audrey took one look over the wooden railing and felt a little dizzy.

"This is lovely," she said as the waiter opened a menu and set it on her lap. A gentle breeze caressed her face. "A very nice choice."

G beamed and pointed to the menu. "Get the *spiedini*. You won't be disappointed."

"*Spiedini*?"

"Veal rolls," he explained. "Delicious."

"Oh, okay," she said, closing her menu and handing it to him. "You know what? I'm going to place myself in your hands, unreservedly. You've never steered me wrong before."

G's eyes gleamed and he rubbed his hands together greedily. He clearly was up to the challenge. When the waiter arrived, G instructed him, occasionally gesturing to Audrey, but using words she'd never heard before. When the waiter nodded and headed off, she laughed. "I have no idea what I'm in for."

"Cow spleen. I hope you like it," he said with a wink.

She nearly gagged. "Serious?"

21

"No. I'm easing you into the cuisine. We will save the *pani ca meusa* for later! It's good. You cannot miss."

"I'll have you know that I ate sea urchins in Lipari, and they were actually delicious," she said proudly.

"Ah, *Pasta con i Ricci di Mare?* That is impressive," he said.

"Nothing can be better than your *arancini* and *ciambotta*, though!" She laughed and looked out over the town. The sun was just setting behind some darker clouds in the distance, creating a display of color and light that even fireworks could not rival. She gazed at it and smiled. As she did, her eyes fell down upon the orange groves, below. The smells of delicious food from the bistro overpowered that of the citrus, but from this vantage, the view of the estate was even better.

Still, there was no sign of life to be seen. It was hard to believe anyone lived there now, because it was just as closed up as it'd always been.

The conversation had lapsed a bit, so she said, "Did you hear the rumors?"

He laughed, and when he did, she realized what a stupid question it was. G had *always* heard the rumors, even before they became rumors. He knew everything about this town. In fact, he probably knew that she was scheduled to go out with Mason tomorrow. Maybe he was just waiting for her to tell him that on her own. Maybe he didn't care.

Why was this all so confusing?

"I heard from several people that mafia moved into that mansion down there. Is that what you heard?"

She nodded.

He shook his head. *"E io sono stufo marcio di tutta questa assurdità!"*

"What?" Her Italian had been getting better, but sometimes, G talked so fast, she couldn't understand him, even when he spoke English.

"I said that it is nonsense." He laughed some more. "It's a rumor that Councilman Falco and others like to float about, now and then, but it is full of the horse manure. *Cosa Nostra* is based in Palermo. They were all but decimated in the 1990s. And yes, their numbers might growing in small cells outside of the city. But they know better than to set up shop in our little one-horse town. *Ricorda le mie parole,* Audrey . . ."

22

The waiter came with a glass of wine. She took a sip of it, letting it relax her nerves. "What does that mean?"

"I said you should listen to me. It'll all turn out to be nothing, in the end."

"You really think so?"

"Of course, of course. If you know anything about the mafia, you know they need to be where the action is. There is nothing here for them."

"Luigi seemed to think it was something worth worrying about. He was issuing all sorts of warnings about associating with them. Have you ever had any dealings with the mafia here?"

He shook his head. "No. But while I agree that you don't want to get tangled up with them, I don't think you'll ever be given the chance." He looked over the railing at the estate, which was now dark. There wasn't a single light coming from the location of the mansion, at all. "This town likes to come up with all sorts of wild rumors. Keeps things interesting. But most of them aren't real. Just stuff to keep the gossip mills churning and keep people talking."

Just then, the food came. The plate in front of her had to have been the veal rolls, and it smelled so wonderful that her mouth watered. She dug in—her knife sliced right through it like warm butter-- and took a bite. The Romano cheese, breadcrumbs, parsley, and garlic all melded together in a way that immediately made her want to take another bite. And another. In fact, she could've inhaled it all at once. "Mmm. This is delicious. You're right."

"I know," he said, and when she looked up at him, she realized he was sipping his wine, watching her, his food untouched. She'd already scarfed down three bites.

"Aren't you going to eat?"

"I was just enjoying watching you enjoy your food. You're beautiful, *Principessa*. Anyone ever tell you that?"

No, no one had, except G. But he was such a charmer. She'd never met anyone like him. Someone who was loved by everyone, who had so much adoration, and yet somehow, he was captivated by *her*, as awkward and ill-at-ease as she could sometimes be. Most people like him flocked together, but she was his opposite in so many ways.

It was a good match, she had to admit. He could give her confidence, and she could . . . well, she wasn't sure what she could give him. But did it matter? From the gleam in his eye, he clearly liked her.

23

So she decided that if this was a date, she was going to grab the bull by the horns and milk it for everything she could. She set her fork down and took a gulp of wine. "Hey. Do you want to dance?"

He nodded and led her out to the dance floor. This time, the floor was nearly empty, as the tarantella had ended, and a slow folk song was playing. G took her hand and wrapped a hand around her waist, and lead her around the floor effortlessly, so much so that she didn't even have to worry. He was a competent dancer. His eyes twinkled. "Not so bad, eh?"

She smiled. "No. Not at all."

In fact, in the moonlight, under the twinkling fairy lights, she felt as if they were far away from everyone else, as if it was just the two of them. A year ago, she never would've believed this would be her life—dancing under the stars with a handsome Sicilian, a world away from the Boston home where she'd grown up.

This is really nice, she thought, as the music slowed down, leaving them lingering, still clinging to one another in the center of the floor. She thought that he'd break apart from her and lead her back to the table.

But he held tight to her, his eyes locked on hers. Then, he started to lean in, closer . . . closer . . .

And instead of closing her eyes and waiting for the kiss, a terrible thing happened.

She thought of Mason.

She stiffened and pulled away, rubbing her bare upper arms. "Oooh, it's getting cold, isn't it?" she asked, looking away.

"Well, it's—"

"Let's go back so I can get my wrap, all right?' she said, heading awkwardly toward the table.

"Of course," he said, following her.

When she sat down and he looked at her across the candlelit table, there was confusion in his eyes. Obviously. *For the last time, Audrey, stop bouncing back and forth! You're going to need to make up your mind, soon, before you hurt someone.*

He took her hand and massaged it gently, sending shivers up her arm. "You are under some stress, is that it?"

She nodded and drained her glass. Tomorrow. She'd make the decision tomorrow.

She had to get to work early, check on Bambino, and then, of course, there was the matter of her other date.

Yes. Tomorrow, everything would be clearer.

CHAPTER FIVE

When Audrey walked into the clinic the following morning, she found Concetta, lying across a couple of hard plastic chairs in the reception area, snoring loudly. The poor girl was twisted into such an unnatural position, Audrey felt a crick in her neck, just looking at her.

Concetta didn't even stir when the door shut. Audrey smiled sadly. *I should let her sleep. And maybe I should look into turning the back supply room into a bedroom for the overnight staff. Mason would probably love to whip that room into a . . .*

She groaned. No thinking of Mason. Or G. Or anyone male. She had bigger things on her mind.

She went into the back room, stopping first to check on Bambino. Right away, she saw why Concetta likely hadn't slept well. The poor pup was sleeping now, but he'd clearly had a rough night. He felt warm, and his heart rate was too rapid. Concetta was efficient and clean, but the area around Bambino's crate looked like a war zone, with discarded paper towels and ripped newspaper everywhere. The scent of pine cleaner only partially masked the stench of vomit.

Maybe it isn't an allergy, she said, petting the dog's small side. *What else? Intestinal blockage? Or something entirely unrelated to the pinecone? It looks like poisoning, but from what?*

She went through, checking all of his other vitals. Unfortunately, he was no better than when he'd been brought in, and the thought made Audrey feel sad and powerless. Her job was to know, to fix things. There was nothing she liked less than having to tell an owner that she didn't know what was wrong with their beloved pet.

Maybe I should call Dr. Carey, she thought, thinking of her last supervisor, the Medical Director of the Back Bay Animal Hospital in Boston. Though Audrey had walked out on that job, Dr. Carey had been one of the good vets there. She'd been in practice at least two decades longer than Audrey, so she'd likely seen a lot more. The last time they'd spoken, months ago, Dr. Carey had told her not to hesitate to call if she needed anything.

No. This is your practice. You can figure this out yourself.

She decided to draw blood and send it in for some tests. Then, she'd have to call Bambino's owner and tell her that he wouldn't be released today. As she was working on getting the materials ready, Concetta wandered into the room, yawning. Despite what must've been an awful night's sleep, she looked as fresh-faced as a skin cleanser ad. "How was your date?" she asked, her eyes falling on Audrey's face. "Oh my God. Did you two get in a punching match?"

Audrey shook her head. "That was from renovations, not the date. It hardly hurts at all," she lied. It'd given her a terrible headache last night. Or maybe that was the wine, or the decision she'd soon have to make.

"Okay. So the date with G?"

"It was very nice," she said, motioning to the dog. "What—"

"That sounds very anticlimactic, Doctor!" she said with a pout. "Was it that bad?"

"No! It was . . . like I said, nice. Now, what happened here?"

"Oh, he was up all night, just whimpering in pain. I don't think the shot did anything for him," she said, reaching into the kibble bucket to start filling the food trays. "But at least he's resting now and seems to be comfortable. I'm hoping he'll just pass whatever it was in his stool today. So tell me how the date went! I want details! Is he the one?"

Audrey frowned. She'd rather talk about the dog's poop.

"I don't know. Maybe. I guess I'll know better after I go out with Mason, tonight." She shuddered. "I know I should be feeling weird about it, but I do. I feel like I'm being deceptive."

Concetta opened a kennel filled with kittens and took one out, stroking it as she held it to her chest. "You're not being deceptive! You're being careful. And don't worry—there is no wrong decision. You don't have to worry about G. I told you, my dad knew his dad. He comes from a good family. He's good looking and successful and everyone just loves him. He is like a big teddy bear!" Then she licked her lips. "But that American . . . yum."

Audrey wrinkled her nose. "Mason is . . . okay."

"Come on! He's so dreamy. I do not think I have ever seen a man that good looking, even on television." She giggled.

Audrey finished extracting the blood and shook her head. "You know, you don't have to stay around here. Go home and get some sleep." *And stop hounding me about the two men I vowed not to think about today.*

27

"All right, all right," she said. "But I'll be back tonight so you can go on your big date! What time is it, anyway?"

"Seven," she muttered, wondering how awkward she'd be with Mr. Dreamy. Even if she was doing no wrong, this two-timing was exhausting.

"I'll be back at six!" she said, grabbing her sweater off the hook by the door. As she did, the phone began to ring. "I'll get that, first."

"Thanks," Audrey called as she went to check on the bunnies. Six of them. She'd gotten them a few weeks ago, and now they were just about ready to be put up for adoption. The little bundles crowded around each other, twitching their noses, nibbling the fresh hay she supplied.

A few moments later, when Audrey was sure she had left, Concetta called to her from the reception desk. "Hey, Dr. Smart? I think you should take this."

That didn't sound good. "What is it?" she called back. Rather than wait for an answer, she decided to find out herself. She picked up the line from the phone in the kennel room and said, "Dr. Smart."

"Doctor?" the low, gravelly voice of someone who'd smoked too many cigarettes said. The person also sounded far away, as if they were speaking in a wind tunnel.

"Yes, speaking. Can I help you?"

"You're the new American doctor who just moved into Mussomeli, right?"

"Right," Audrey said, suspicious, now. The voice sounded more male than female, but it felt eerie that this person knew so much about her, when she knew virtually nothing about them. "What can I help you with . . . I'm sorry, who am I speaking with?"

"I uh," the voice rasped. "I uh, prefer to remain anonymous."

Audrey felt goosebumps popping up on her arms. There was something wrong and sinister about the man's voice. "Do you have an issue with an animal that I can help you with?" she repeated, now just as exasperated as she was creeped out.

"Yes . . . yes. There is an injured animal outside of town."

"Animal. What kind?"

"I don't know."

"It's not yours?"

"No. No it's not. I don't know where it went. But it's somewhere in the orange groves. You know the place?"

Orange groves. The estate. Audrey gripped the phone tighter. "I do. But that's a very large place. You'll have to be a little more specific than that if you want me to track down—"

"Just follow the trail of blood."

Then the line went dead.

Audrey stood there, stiff, listening to the utter silence, replaying the speaker's words in her head: *Just follow the trail of blood.*

It sounded like something from a horror flick.

She was so freaked out about it that she didn't notice someone entering behind her. When a hand fell on her shoulder, she jumped nearly to the ceiling.

Then she spun, ready to lash out with a right hook. She stopped mid-punch.

"Concetta!"

Her eyes were wide. She patted a hand against her heaving chest, clearly as surprised as Audrey was. "What! I thought you heard me!"

"No! I was on the phone. I thought you left."

"Sorry. But that was creepy, wasn't it? He sounded like a heavy breather. Was it a crank call?"

Audrey nodded. "No, but it was super creepy. Did he say anything to you?"

"No, other than that he wanted to talk to the veterinarian because he had an emergency. But he sounded like he was gasping for air. I thought he was dying, himself. What did he say to you?"

"He said there's some injured animal in the orange groves and I have to follow a trail of blood to get to it," she said. "I think that's how most horror movies start."

"Wow. Are you going? If you are, you shouldn't go alone!"

Audrey grabbed her medicine bag and shrugged. "I don't think I really have a choice. If there's an animal in need, I've got to go to it," she said, looking around the clinic, her eyes landing on poor Bambino. "I guess this little guy will be okay if I'm gone an hour, max."

"I'll stay with him," Concetta volunteered.

"Oh, no!" Audrey said, though she had to admire the woman's enthusiasm. But she'd gone above and beyond. "I feel like I'm taking advantage of you. I can't ask you to—"

"Stop. I want to."

"Then fine. I guess I'll have an excuse to miss out on the date with Mason, then, to—"

29

"No. You. Don't!" she said, jabbing her finger at Audrey. "You're going to that, too. I'm going to make sure it happens, if I have to drag you to his front door myself."

"All right, fine!" Audrey said with a frown as she headed to the door. "There are no appointments this morning, anyway. So please, chill as much as you can. Order breakfast in. My treat. I'll be back as soon as I can."

As she headed out the door, she saw Nick, waiting patiently for her. "Hey there, just the fox I was hoping to see," she said to him, hurrying down the street as he stayed close to her heels. "Want to come with me and use that nose of yours? An animal is in trouble. Let's go and find it."

CHAPTER SIX

The rolling hills of orange groves looked lovely and picturesque from her bedroom window, stretching on and on, in perfect rows.

But once she was on the street, outside them, Audrey realized it was more like a jungle. A vast, dark, frightening one. As in, *People go in, but they don't ever go out.*

As she stared at it, a bird cawed overhead, a raven of death, singing out a warning. She put the heat index at eighty, maybe ninety, since her shirt was already drenched with sweat, even after the short walk down the hill, to the grove. Going back up would be hell. A fly or mosquito nipped at her neck, and she smacked it, then studied her fingertips. A gross black insect body and blood stained her fingers. She wiped it on her shorts and looked down at Nick. "Ready, Bub?"

He was already padding around the soft grass on the shoulder of the road, sniffing with interest.

It was *Audrey* who didn't feel ready. She'd asked for more definite directions because she knew how massive this place was, but now, finding anything within these thousands of trees seemed like folly. The orange tree leaves rustled in the breeze above her, and the sunlight slashing through made strange shapes on the ground, making it difficult to see anything at all. Though the sun was bright, it felt eerie, knowing what she was here for. She didn't even know where to start searching for the trail of blood. And Nick might've had a nose, but he wasn't *that* good.

All right, whatever, she said as she took a step and felt another little insect climb under her shirt, skirting down her collarbone. The feeling was both ticklish and terrifying. She swatted and looked down. This time, no doubt about it, it was a mosquito.

"I am going to look like one giant mosquito bite for my date with Mason," she muttered under her breath as she stepped through the grass. "He's gonna love me."

If you even make it out alive! A sinister voice inside her said. One that sounded remarkably like the man on the phone. He'd had very little

Italian in his accent, but he hadn't sounded American, either . . . he'd sounded almost otherworldly.

Yes, this would be the part where the unknowing stupid girl traipsed off alone, into certain disaster.

In the shade of the trees, she walked down one row as long as she could, following Nick, who seemed to be on the scent of something. All she could smell were oranges—the scent was so thick here that it was almost overpowering. Not unpleasant in the least, but still, the hair on the back of her neck stood up.

After a few minutes, Nick stopped, looked around, sniffed again, and tore off in a direction perpendicular to the route they'd started taking.

"Wait!" she called, rushing after him. If she lost him in this, she'd probably never find him again. The place was huge. When she turned around to check the way she'd come, she could no longer see the road. *I wish I had a compass. Does my phone have a compass?*

She pulled it out and started fingering through the apps. No such luck. Then she turned on the Maps app and tried to see if that was any help. Nope. It put her in the middle of an empty orange blob.

I am going to get screwed, I'll bet, she thought, imagining herself becoming so hopelessly lost in the grove that she wound up getting her only sustenance from oranges and then being found, a veritable skeleton, months later. She'd read news stories about people who trekked into the wilderness on a simple day-hike, only to be found months later, delirious shadows of their former selves.

That can very well be me. Of course, with all this Vitamin C, I probably won't have a cold, she thought, ducking under a branch of a tree and turning her head this way and that, hoping to spot Nick.

Nothing. He was gone.

"Urgh," she growled, bending over to slip under a low-hanging branch. As she did, her head began to pound again. That awful welt had eventually settled on a sunrise pink, with a bit of purple, that even concealer hadn't been able to hide. When she moved her head too fast, she also felt dizzy, which was why her vision swam as she straightened. She spun around, getting even more hopelessly lost.

"Nick!" She whispered it, because she was aware she was probably trespassing. Also, if the rumors were true and the Tivoli Estate had been sold to the mafia, who knew what kind of security they had? Probably big, burly men who ripped people limb from limb merely for looking at them the wrong way. Trespassing? She'd probably disappear, never to be seen again.

She didn't want to end this day, sleeping with the fishes. That would really put a damper on things.

Good thing there was no one around. It seemed like she was the only person about for miles. The mansion itself wasn't visible from here. In fact, she hadn't seen a single soul since she left the town proper.

Pushing her hair back into a ponytail, which said she meant business, she walked up another row, looking for anything that could even resemble blood. How would she even follow a trail of blood? The grass was thick, blowing in the breeze. The ground was uneven. This was like finding a bloodstain in a haystack.

I bet it was a crank call, she told herself once she came out on a clearing. She whirled around in a three-sixty, getting nervous. *Now I guess I need to find out where I am, and how to get out of here.*

Easier said than done. In every direction, the scenery was the same: acres and acres of lush orange trees. Her pulse skittered as she looked up, trying to find the sun, as if that might give her a clue. But it seemed to slash down through the branches, from everywhere, hiding its true location in the sky.

She walked to the middle of the clearing, still trying to determine which way to go. There was a large rock there, so she climbed atop it and looked around, shielding her eyes from the sun, which was now straight overhead. As she spun, she saw the tops of trees, the tile roof of the villa in the distance, but absolutely no sign of life whatsoever.

Except . . .

She squinted when she noticed a flash of red among the trees. It wasn't animal, for sure, unless the animals around here had taken to wearing clothing. It was too big to be simply a collar. She looked closer, making out an arm, and legs.

Human arms and legs. Someone was walking in the grove, weaving through the trees. From the position of the red, over the person's arms, she assumed it was a hat. Maybe a scarf. The red was in a polka-dotted pattern, bright and gaudy.

Hat or scarf, that is the ugliest piece of clothing I've ever seen. But whatever. Maybe whoever that is knows the way out! I'm saved!

She slipped from the rock and followed after the figure, but then thought better of it. Luigi had been pretty serious when he spoke of the

Sicilian mafia. He'd told her not to get tangled up with them. And what if this person was mafia? What if he wasn't happy to see her? What if he shot her for trespassing?

She stared after the form until it disappeared from view. When it did, she realized her hands were slick with sweat. She wiped them on the sides of her shorts and scratched at something on her hand. A bump rose up as she did.

Perfect. Another mosquito bite. I am so blessed to have sweet blood. Mason will love the way I look . . . if I ever get out of here to make it to our date.

She checked her phone. It was almost noon. She had to get back and relieve poor Concetta, who'd been working far too hard, and too much.

"Nick!" she called in a hushed whisper.

Nothing.

The moment she straightened, thinking that subsisting on oranges for the next few weeks was her future, a shadow descended over her, and a heavy hand fell upon her shoulder.

CHAPTER SEVEN

"What the—"

Audrey jumped, then stumbled backwards, sure she'd see a man in sunglasses and a zoot suit, with a machine gun. For some reason, when she thought mafia, that was the first thing that popped into her mind. Ridiculous, she knew.

It seemed even more ridiculous as she found herself falling backwards. Her feet slipped out from under her, and she was just about to hit the ground when a strong, tanned hand reached out and grabbed her wrist, yanking her forward.

She came face-to-chest with an impossibly tall, built man in a white linen shirt, rolled up to the elbows. In her shock, she inhaled sharply, catching the manly smell of soap and leather over the sweet scent of citrus.

"Easy, now," he said, as she looked way up into two impossibly dark eyes. Chestnut hair curled romantically around his face, making him look like a statue of David. "I'm sorry if I frightened you."

"Oh, I uh . . ." A thousand thoughts flooded her mind, but of those, one battled its way to the forefront. "You speak English? How did you know . . ."

He chuckled, and with barely an accent, said, "You were muttering to yourself in English."

"Ah." Her face flamed. *Was I? Probably.* "I was looking for something."

"Something?" He stroked his strong chin as she looked down, unable to meet his eyes. He was wearing khakis, loafers and a heavy, expensive-looking wristwatch. Definitely not the attire one would wear, working in the grove. "Can I help you find it?"

"I don't—" She stopped, thinking of Luigi's words. No, this man didn't look like typical mafia from the movies. But that didn't mean he wasn't one. Still, the whole town was curious about the Tivoli estate's new owners. It'd be nice to have first-hand knowledge to contribute to them. "Is this your place?"

He nodded. "I just moved in."

"Oh. Well, welcome," she said awkwardly, still unable to meet his eyes. Not only that; he seemed to radiate something, a warmth, that magnetized her. *Goodness, he's handsome.*

The farthest up she could look was at his chin. One corner of his mouth lifted up, baring a dimple. He said, "Something tells me you are not the welcoming committee. They usually come to the front door. They don't sneak around the grounds."

"Oh." *Why am I saying "Oh" after everything he says?* "No, I didn't mean to be sneaking. You see, I'm the town's veterinarian."

"You are?" He seemed doubtful. Of course, most people were. Audrey barely looked a day over eighteen, with her freckles and baby face. It didn't seem possible that she could be a full-fledged doctor of veterinary medicine.

"Yes. I am. And I received a call at my clinic. Someone said they thought an animal had been injured out here. They said to follow the trail of blood."

"Blood, huh?" He looked around. "Well, I haven't seen or heard anything, and I've been walking about the grove all morning."

"Oh," she said, grimacing when she realized she'd said "oh" again. "Well, it was probably just a crank call then. I'll just be . . ." She pointed behind her, even though she wasn't really sure that was the way out.

"Who's Nick?"

She stared at him. *What is he, a psychic?*

"You were calling for Nick," he explained in response to her confusion.

"Oh, uh. Nick's my pet. A fox. He seems to have run off."

"Ah. I understand." He looked around. "I don't see him now."

"No. Neither do I. But he'll find his way back eventually."

"You are a very compassionate woman. You like the world's creatures, I see."

"Uh . . . yes. Goes with the job, I guess."

"Nonsense. You wouldn't have become one if you didn't have that special trait. It's admirable, for you to come all this way, based on a rumor. You're a caring soul."

"T-thank you," she stammered, drawing her toe through the grass at her feet. *What is wrong with me? You'd think I'd be used to dealing with handsome men, by now. Apparently not.* She took a step back. "Well, it was nice meeting you. I'll see myself . . ."

36

"I don't think we did."

She froze. *Did what?* She managed a look up at his eyes, trying to gauge his intent, but it only served to make her feel even more hypnotized by him. "I'm sorry?"

"Meet." He thrust a hand out to her. "I'm Rafael."

Rafael. It even sounded sexy. She blushed as she touched his hand, shaking just his fingertips. There was no electricity, because her hands were too slick with sweat. Also, there were probably some dead bug guts on them, as well. "Audrey. Audrey Smart."

"Nice to meet you. Now, we can say we have met."

He didn't let go of her hand, right away. It seemed like he was lost in thought, for a moment. Audrey really hoped that this wasn't a mistake. *Best to not get wrapped up with them.* Now, he knew her name.

Oh, stop it, Audrey. He's probably not mafia. G said it was ridiculous, that rumors like that always went around. You're fine.

Before he dropped her hand, he said, "Doctor Smart, I was just about to have lunch in my courtyard. Would you be interested in joining me?"

She blinked. Her hair was in a ponytail and she was sweaty. She hadn't been planning on a lunch date. Plus, did she really want to add to the number of times she "oh"-ed around this man? And what if he was mafia? Not to mention that she'd told Concetta she'd be back soon to relieve her.

"Well, I should get going back to my—"

"Ah. Stay for lunch. I know no one here, and I'm eager for the company. Just a few minutes." He smiled. "I can drive you back to your clinic when we are done. How is that?"

She smiled. "I guess. Sure. Thanks. Sounds great."

*

After climbing a set of crumbling stone stairs, Rafael opened a rustic iron gate through an archway, leading her into a vast rectangular courtyard, filled with cypress trees and terra cotta pots filled with colorful flowers. The floor was a gleaming river stone, and there was a fountain in the center of it with a Roman statue of a woman holding a vase. Audrey marveled at the beauty of the old home. *I wonder what it looks like inside.*

37

He motioned to a small bistro table near the fountain. "Sit, sit," he said, pulling out a small, spindly iron-backed chair. "Can I interest you is some Prosecco?"

"Yes. Sure," she said, eyes volleying around the place, looking for something that said, *I am mafia.*

Of course, there was nothing, unless you counted the well-appointed, clearly expensive home. No machine guns lying about. No sinister-looking, stoic brothers standing in the shadows. She shivered as she realized she'd just walked into this strange man's home, alone. Even if he wasn't mafia, that could be dangerous.

"I'm sorry if the place is a bit of a mess. Just moving in and all. It's been shuttered for over a year, unfortunately," he said, looking around in dismay. Then he called, "Marta!"

A plump, grandmotherly woman in a black service outfit appeared. "Si?"

"Dacci una bottiglia di De Luca. E porta il pranzo per me e la mia amica," he said effortlessly, much to Audrey's surprise. He'd spoken English so well that she'd nearly forgotten he was likely Sicilian.

The woman nodded and scurried off.

He sat across from her and smiled. "Much to be done, still. But we will get this place back to its former glory."

"What brings you to Mussomeli?" Audrey asked, venturing to look in his eyes. Nope. Not quite yet.

"I was tired from the busyness of Palermo. This place has been in my family for years. I inherited it from family."

Audrey frowned. "I thought it was for sale?"

"It was. I'd planned to sell. But then my circumstances—they changed. I wanted someplace quiet to lay—to settle, you see," he said as Marta arrived with an *antipasti* full of olives, cheeses, salami, bread, and artichokes. She poured them each a glass of wine and bowed slightly. Rafael flicked her off, as if he'd been used to dealing with servants all his life, then sipped his wine. "Mussomeli fits the bill."

Wait, did he just say he was looking for a place to lie low? Audrey stared at him, so distracted by his words that she almost missed the stem of her wine glass when she reached for it and wound up knocking it over. She successfully recovered and took a sip.

"I hope you like *involtini di pesce spade,"* he said. "It's Marta's specialty. She makes the best I've ever had."

"I don't know what that is."

38

"Swordfish rolls, covered in breadcrumbs. You'll like it, if you like fish."

"I do. I'm sure I'll like it," she said, looking over the antipasti. She took a tiny piece of bread and nibbled on it. It was hard to believe there was another course after this; she usually just skipped lunch for work or scarfed down an apple in the back room of the clinic.

"And of course, Marta makes the best *granita d'arincia,* for dessert." He popped an olive into his mouth. "So, how is it you came to live here, beautiful American lady?"

She blushed hot. "I got taken in by the one-dollar house scheme."

"Taken in?"

She laughed. "No, I don't mean that. It hasn't been bad. It's just been a lot of work, because the town needed a vet clinic right away. So I've been handling renovations on my place and setting up a clinic. It's been pretty hectic."

"I see. I heard that there was a bit of a stray problem here. How is the town treating you?"

"Oh, fine. Everyone's really nice. And understanding of my terrible Italian. Plus, there are expats from all over the world coming here. It's definitely been an adventure," she said, looking around. A breeze blew her hair in front of her face, and she had the strangest feeling, like she was being watched.

"When did you get here?"

"A few months ago. It's definitely been busy. But I love the town and its people. You grew up around here? You said the place was in your family?"

He shook his head. "Palermo. But yes. It came from my family."

Family. That was kind of broad and vague. She had to wonder if he was being that way on purpose. "You live here alone? Why?"

He chuckled. "I suppose you can say I haven't found the right woman yet."

She nearly choked on her Prosecco. "Oh, no. I just meant that it's a big place for just one."

He leaned forward and tented his hands in front of him. "I suppose you can say I like to spread out. And I value my privacy."

So it was probably not a good idea that you were infringing on it, Audrey, she thought, stiffening. This was where, in the mafia movies, he'd pull a sleek pistol from under the table. She'd plead, "I didn't know! I'll be more careful next time!" And he'd say, "There won't be a next time," before coolly blowing her away.

But of course, he didn't do any of that. He simply grabbed his napkin and laid it over his lap. "Ah. You're in for a treat. Dr. Smart!"

The food came. It smelled lightly of seafood, but nuttier, like the toasted breadcrumbs. Audrey's mouth began to water at the sight of the golden-fried rolls. "It looks delicious."

It *tasted* delicious, too. She took a bite, letting the flavors meld on her tongue. "Wow," she said. "This is good. So this place has been in your family a long time? It's old, isn't it? It must have a history."

"Yes, the Tivoli estate was the refuge of an Italian princess, Chiara Tivoli, who fled to Sicily to avoid the Nazi regime. She'd been charged with working against the war effort. She was later captured and brought to a concentration camp. My great-great grandfather came to know her, there, and somehow, upon her death, the estate came into his name."

"Somehow?"

He laughed. "I can't say I'm very well-versed in the details." He pointed to the fountain, where she could see a dolphin inlaid in mosaic tiles. "Those tiles are imported from the mainland, as were the Roman columns. They're centuries old."

She smiled. By the time she finished her food, she knew a lot about the home, but very little about the man that sat across from her. Also, she'd had maybe one too many glasses of Prosecco, because when lunch ended and she tried to stand up, she felt dizzy and light, like she might be able to fly away. "Oh," she said, and blinked.

"Are you alright?"

She waved him away, even as she wavered on her feet. Looking around, she wondered where Nick had gone, and if he was still tooling around the orange groves. "Perfect. Just fine."

But was she? She gulped a breath of air and blinked some more, trying to get the swirling courtyard into focus. The scenery around her spun. Much more of this, and she wasn't sure she'd be able to keep her swordfish down.

"Come this way. My car is over here," he said, motioning to her.

He probably had a Ferrari. Or a Lamborghini. Something that probably cost more money than she'd seen in her life. She could just imagine throwing up all over his leather upholstery. "No, that's all right," she said, looking around. "If you point me in the right direction, I'll walk. The fresh air will do me good."

"Are you sure?"

She nodded, pointing out a door. "This way?"

He pointed in an entirely opposite direction. "That way. There is a shortcut straight to town if you're willing to climb a few stairs. Just stay to the right."

"Oh. That's fine." She giggled. All the doors looked the same. "Thanks. And thank you for the lovely meal."

He stood up, coming almost uncomfortably close to her. That was one thing she hadn't gotten used to about Sicily—people were used to far less personal space, so they often got right in her face when they talked to her. But as he put his hands on her shoulder, she couldn't remember any other Sicilian ever getting *this* close.

Then he leaned over, and very gently gave her a kiss on each cheek. "It has been a pleasure, lovely doctor," he said in a low voice with a timbre that melted her insides. "'Til we meet again?"

She nodded goofily, then turned and almost walked straight into the fountain. She giggled through the pain as her shins collided with the marble enclosure. "Whoops."

Collecting herself, she waved at him again and tottered off, through the gate and out of the courtyard. Sure enough, she saw a gravel pathway heading off toward the right. Beyond that, past some trees and brush, there was a staircase cut into a cliffside that might as well have been a ladder. Audrey stared at it, getting a little dizzy, just thinking about climbing those flights.

I don't know if I can do this.

She turned around and looked at the mansion. She could ask Rafael for that ride, but then again, she'd already embarrassed herself enough for one day.

Come on. It's like they always tell you—just don't look down. It'll be fine.

Squaring her shoulders, she took a few steps down the path.

But that was when she saw it.

A few small, dark spots, scattered among the gravel.

She leaned over, then crouched to get a better look, almost pitching forward in her tipsiness. As she got closer, she saw the definite deep crimson tinge and confirmed it. Blood.

She looked around and noticed another few blood drops, heading out toward the orange grove.

It was the blood trail the caller had told her about.

So it hadn't been a crank. Jumping up, now feeling more sober, she took off, looking for the wounded animal. She found more blood as she went, some droplets on the grass, some smeared on the tree trunks. Poor animal. It was a wonder it hadn't bled out. Maybe it had.

She scanned the ground in front of her, following the trail, but then, it simply ended. She stopped under the shade of a tree and caught her breath, wishing she had a glass of water. She also kind of had to pee. But it seemed that the animal had just disappeared into thin air.

Sighing, she went around a tree to head back to the staircase when she stumbled over something big and dark, lying in the grass. A rock. She fell with an "oof!", the pain ripping through her knees.

Rolling onto her backside, she looked at the grass stains on her knees. One of them was scratched and raw, starting to bleed. "Great," she mumbled, reaching into her medical bag and pulling out a band-aid. "Pays to come prepared."

She started to put it on, but decided it needed antiseptic. She had that, too. She dabbed a little on a cotton ball and gently dabbed it on the wound as something moved in the grass. It jumped up, sitting on the rock in front of her.

"Oh, there you are, Nick," she said, glancing up at him. "I thought you were going to help me find . . ."

She froze.

Because Nick wasn't sitting on a rock.

He was sitting on just the thing she'd sent him out to find. A wounded animal.

Only this wasn't a wounded animal. It was a man in a black suit, and from his face-down position, as still as he was, she was pretty sure "wounded" was an understatement. He was dead.

CHAPTER EIGHT

Audrey sat on a stone wall at the edge of the street, waiting for the police to arrive and fanning her face, trying to keep calm. She sat there, at the edge of the property, which was quite far away from the body she'd found, so she could direct Detective Dinardo to the scene of the crime. Which was fine with her, because she didn't want to be there, with *him*.

Whoever he was.

Detective Dinardo was Mussomeli's only detective, a no-nonsense, hard-edged man who rarely smiled. He was probably mid-forties, with a scarred, weathered face of someone who'd had a lot of trials in life. When he pulled up to her, he rolled his eyes through the windshield. Then he pushed open the door. "You again, Dr. Smart?"

She shrugged helplessly. "Hello to you, too, Detective." The truth was that she'd already found three other bodies in town and was starting to get a complex. "I don't understand. I guess I'm just unlucky."

"I'll say. If you stay in Mussomeli much longer, we might start having a population problem," he muttered. "You said you found a body?"

She motioned behind her. Now, she was almost completely sober, and getting a migraine. "If you keep following this row of trees closer to the house, you'll find him. I think he's been shot."

Detective Dinardo silently headed off to the scene as another police car pulled up. This time, Officer Ricci, the buff young police officer stepped out. He started laughing. "*Dottore* Smart!" He slapped his knee. "Not you again!"

"Yes, it's me," she mumbled, looking up at the sun. It was starting to dip behind the cliffs. Poor Concetta was probably wondering what happened to her.

Officer Ricci came over to her and handed her a cold bottle of water. Eureka. She took a drink from it, deciding he probably didn't have a porta-potty socked away in his little cruiser. "Thank you so much."

43

He motioned down the path. "What is it?"

"Another murder, I think." She shuddered. "Actually, I know. Unless there's a way a guy could commit suicide by shooting himself in the back."

Ricci raised an eyebrow. "Wow." Audrey couldn't tell if he was shocked or excited. He climbed the short stone fence and headed in the same direction as Dinardo.

After a few moments, Audrey decided to follow. She arrived just as Dinardo was kneeling in front of the body. "Looks like he's been dead a few hours." He looked up at Ricci. "Call in the coroner."

Ricci nodded and pulled out his radio, then headed off.

Dinardo continued to survey the body. "Looks like he was shot twice at close range," he said, running a finger over the bullet wounds between the body's shoulder blades. He looked up at Audrey, whose stomach was now turning. "Which reminds me, what were you doing here?"

"Well, I—"

"What seems to be the problem here?" a voice said from among the trees. A moment later, Rafael appeared.

Dinardo straightened. "A body was found on these premises. Who are you?"

Rafael tilted his head and looked, unsurprised, at the dead body. "I own this place." He extended his hand and smiled good-naturedly. "Rafael."

Dinardo shook it cautiously.

Audrey waited for Rafael to say the next, obvious question. *Who is it?* After all, if someone was found dead on her property, the first thing she'd register is shock. Then, she'd want to know if it was anyone she was close to. After that, she'd probably ask what happened.

But Rafael said absolutely nothing.

From the way Dinardo looked at him, Audrey got the feeling he was suspicious of this, too. He said, "You're new here, eh?"

"I moved in last week," he said. "It's my family property. And before you ask where I was at the time of the murder, I was here at my estate. No, I did not hear or see anything. So no, I'm afraid I can't help you very much at all."

Audrey just stared. Rafael spoke coolly, as if it was some discarded trash that had been found on his property, and not a human body. As if this was the kind of nuisance he'd had to deal with often. And as

44

Audrey let it simmer, she realized something. *Had Dinardo even said it was a murder?*

Dinardo reached into the man's pocket and pulled out a wallet. "Pietro Grinelli," he said, holding up some form of identification. "Either of you know the man?"

They both shook their heads.

Rafael frowned. "No. I trust that you two can take care of this tonight? I don't want to have to deal with this. I came out here for peace and quiet. You understand?"

Dinardo squinted at him. "I'm going to have to question you, Signore . . . what did you say your last name was?"

He rolled his eyes. "I didn't. It's Piccolo."

Audrey tilted her head. Piccolo. Why did that name sound so familiar?

Suddenly, Luigi's voice came to her. *The Piccolo clan is one of the meanest and worst. Cosa Nostra.*

Her jaw dropped. Oh, no. If he was Cosa Nostra, and he had been prowling the orange groves prior to her arriving there, then . . .

He was probably a murderer. He'd probably murdered that man, right before he met her.

She jumped up. "I've got to go!" she shouted. As she said that, she remembered, she really had to pee. So it wasn't a lie.

"Sit right down there," Dinardo ordered. "I have questions to ask you."

"All right. Fine. But I do have to get back to the clinic," she said, sitting on a nearby rock and crossing her legs.

"Ricci, get Dr. Smart's statement. I'll interview Mr. Piccolo, here," he said.

The junior officer fumbled with his pad and pen and smiled his million-dollar smile. "Hi, Dottore Smart. I'm going to ask you some questions," he said.

"Yes. We've established that," she said with a smile. She couldn't fault him. He was still naïve, even after dealing with three other murders. "If we could just . . . move this along?"

"Uh. You got it," he said, looking at his notes. One would've thought he'd be just as practiced with murder investigations as some big-city cops, what with the action Mussomeli was getting as of late. But he scratched his neck, unsure. "So what were you doing here?"

"I received a call from an anonymous person. A man, I think. He told me there was an injured animal out here and to follow the trail of blood."

"I see. And did he give his name?"

"No." She ordinarily would have humored him, but right now, her bladder was calling to her. "Thus, anonymous."

"Right. So you arrived here and uh, what time?"

"Right before noon. I walked around and didn't find anything."

"Did you walk where the body was found?"

"I don't know. It all looked the same. But I don't think so."

"Did you see anyone while you were out there?"

"No one, except Rafael, who invited me to lunch in the courtyard. When I was leaving at one-thirty, I saw the trail of blood and followed it, where I found the dead man, exactly where he is now. I didn't touch the body. I know how this rodeo goes."

"That's good."

"Oh—uh. But I did kind of trip over him. So that might've jostled him around a bit. Sorry."

He scratched the side of his head as he stared at her, and his expression said, *Of course you did.* "And you've never met the guy?"

"Nope. Not that I know of. Like I said, I didn't touch the body, and he's face-down, so I don't really know what he looks like."

"And you . . ." He squinted, trying to think up the next question.

She answered for him. "I didn't hear or see anything. So I'm really not that much help." She went to take a sip of her water, but just then, her bladder started to send her warning signals. She stood up. "If we're done here, I do have to go?"

His normally placid expression gave way to confusion. "Do you have an appointment?"

"I just have to get back to the clinic," she said. *As quickly as possible.*

He closed his notebook. Just when she thought she was free, he held up a finger. "Wait one moment. I have to talk to Dinardo."

He went down the trail, she watched him, wondering if it'd be okay to duck behind a tree. Or maybe she should ask Rafael to use his bathroom. But she couldn't do that. He was mafia. And he'd just murdered a man. Shot him in the back and acted like it was nothing. Surely, Dinardo was finding that out right now, and would arrest him. Or would he? Maybe the Piccolo family had infiltrated the police of

Mussomeli and would cover it up. In fact, that was probably why the two of them had gone off, together, alone. Maybe they were making shady mafia deals.

Whatever. They could do whatever they wanted to. She needed to get out of here, soon, before she had a massively embarrassing problem.

A moment later, Dinardo jogged down the path to her. "Dr. Smart?"

"Yes?" she said, hoping he'd tell her *Nothing to see here,* and politely dismiss her.

"Officer Ricci here says that you've been acting strange? Elusive? Wanting to leave?" he asked. "What seems to be the problem?"

She glanced at Officer Ricci, who was busy studying the sky and pretending they didn't exist. She scowled. "No, I'm not being elusive. If I was being elusive, I wouldn't have called you when I found the body, right?"

"Perhaps, but it seems logical that you might have been walking about, looking for this injured animal, and this man popped out and surprised you. So you shot him."

"In the back?" she asked incredulously. "And with what gun? Detective, I will tell you, I don't own a gun. I don't even know how to shoot a gun. If you're trying to come up with a theory, you'd better try harder than that. If you want, search me. There is no gun."

"It could be anywhere. This grove is acres and acres. You had time to ditch it. Also, Mr. Piccolo said that he wasn't in this area before he noticed you, but that you'd been coming from that direction, and you looked flustered."

"He sneaked up on me!" she said, hardly able to believe she was having this conversation. Again. Every time she called in a murder, the police came after her. Sure, it was suspicious, but it was just her bad luck. Nothing more. "Yes, I got *flustered* when a strange man sneaked up on me. Believe it or not, I didn't pull out the heat I was packing and blow him away."

"Mr. Piccolo said it was strange to find you on his grounds, and that you appeared to be looking for something."

"Yes, well, I told you, I was out looking for that injured animal."

"Which you did not find . . ."

"Right, but . . ." She knew where this was going, and she didn't like it one bit.

"Maybe you made that story up?"

"Why? So I could go into the grove and steal oranges?" she asked with incredulity. "I like citrus, but not that much. I can just buy it at Pepe, you know."

"Hmm," he said, stroking his chin pensively.

How did I get to this point? she wondered miserably. Just an hour ago, she'd been so happy. She'd had a nice, enjoyable lunch, and had even been a little smitten with her host, who'd complimented her up and down, making her feel special. Beautiful.

Now, she was a suspect in a murder. Again.

This was getting old, fast.

And she wasn't sure what worse—that she was kind of smitten with a possible mafia guy, or that he was trying to frame her.

Mafia.

The thought made her shudder. They had very powerful connections, and she was just an expat veterinarian. What chance did she have? "Why aren't you even looking at Rafael Piccolo? He's a strange guy, and this is his property. I hear he's possibly—" she trailed off and looked around. *In mafia movies, even the walls have eyes.*

"You hear he's possibly what?" Dinardo asked, eyes narrowed.

She cupped her hands around her mouth, ready to tell him, but then she remembered what she'd thought earlier, about the mafia having the police in their back pockets. She sighed. "Forget it."

I can't believe this. Mr. It's-a-pleasure-lovely-doctor-lady is actually trying to frame me for a murder he committed. And the police believe the flimsy story he was shilling. This is ridiculous.

But from the look on the local law enforcement's faces, she was in some serious trouble, indeed. They really did believe that she'd shot this man.

"Can I go now?" she asked, her voice barely a whisper.

The detective nodded. "Yes, but don't—"

"I get it. Don't leave town. I've been there before, Detective, remember?" She sighed and turned away from him, motioning to Nick to follow her.

As she walked, she could feel their eyes on her back. She didn't want to make herself look any more guilty than she already did, so she forced herself to walk at a leisurely, nonchalant pace until she was out of their sight, behind the trees.

Then she broke into a run, all the way back to the clinic.

CHAPTER NINE

Concetta was at the front desk of the clinic when Audrey burst in.

"There you are! I was wondering—"

"Wait!" Audrey cried, rushing to the bathroom. She made it just in time, slamming the door and taking care of business. As she washed up, that problem solved, all the other ones seemed to avalanche on top of her.

Another murder.

A possible mafia guy, trying to frame her.

What other stress could she pile on top of that?

The moment she stepped outside, she discovered it. Concetta was waiting out in the hallway. "Bambino's not any better," she said gravely.

Audrey let out a deep sigh and went to the kennel to check him out. As she did, Concetta followed. "You were gone a long time. What happened? Did you find the injured pet?"

She groaned. "What *didn't* happen is more like it," she said as she plucked two gloves from the dispenser and snapped them on. She approached Bambino on his bed. He was awake, but lethargic. Yes, no improvement whatsoever. "And no, I didn't find the injured animal. Instead, I found a dead man. "

Concetta laughed. She must've thought Audrey was joking. When Audrey didn't smile, her jaw dropped. "You're serious?"

"Dead. As was the victim. He'd been shot twice in the back."

Concetta brought her hands to her cheeks. "Oh, my goodness. Who could've done such a thing? Mussomeli doesn't have murderers."

Apparently, over the past few months, they do, she thought, taking her stethoscope and listening to Bambino's slow but steady heart rate. "You sent the blood out for testing?"

Concetta nodded.

"I think, if he's not getting better by tonight, we should get an X-ray in. There could be a bowel obstruction, so we might have to perform surgery and repair the damaged tissue. Have you seen a colorectal resection done before, with intestinal anastomosis?"

She shook her head.

"All right, well, let's hope it doesn't come to that. Let's increase his fluids in preparation," she said, pulling off the gloves.

"About this murder . . ."

"Right. The police think I did it."

She laughed again. "Now, you *have* to be joking."

"Well, when the only other guy who was there is a criminal with big connections to the mob, who else are they going to blame? I'm a patsy," she said, going to the sink and washing her hands again.

Concetta raised both eyebrows. "Connections to the mob?"

"Yeah . . . well, no. Forget I said anything about that," she said. The last thing she needed was for word to somehow get back to those powerful people that she was talking smack about them. "But Concetta . . . you've lived in Sicily all your life. Do you know anything about the mafia?"

She nodded. "There was always talk of the mafia in Palermo. Any crime around there, they were usually involved. Or those were the rumors. Supposedly, that was their home base. But I never saw them. I was removed from all that at the university." She paused. "What does the mafia have to do with all this?"

Audrey shrugged. "Well, I've just heard rumors . . ."

"Oh." Concetta nodded and clapped her hands. "I've heard those, too. About the mob moving into that old place down by the orange groves outside of town? But no one really believed them. Why would the mob move all the way out here?" Her eyes narrowed. "Wait. Are you saying you saw them, and you think they killed the man?"

Audrey shrugged. "I'm not saying anything. All I know is that I don't own and never have owned a gun. I wouldn't even know how to shoot one. I met the owner, yes. He invited me to lunch. He seemed really charming and kind, and he was clearly rich."

"Handsome?" Concetta winked.

"Okay, yes. Handsome. I had a great time."

"And then?"

"Well, then I found the body. And from what he told the police, he's making it seem like *I* killed the man. But I don't see how it could be anyone else but him. Other than his servants, who were in the house, there was probably no one around for . . ." She froze as a memory came to her. "Wait. There was someone else in the grove. Someone wearing a hat, or a scarf, that was white with red polka dots. I forgot to tell the police that."

"Red polka dots? That sounds awful," she said, making a face. "I don't know why anyone would want to wear anything that makes them look like they're breaking out in hives. Could it have been the handsome owner?"

"No. I don't think so. He wasn't wearing anything like that when I bumped into him a few minutes later. But who knows? Maybe he discarded his hat, just like the police think I discarded my gun. Not that I can picture him wearing red polka dots. You're right. It's hideous. He seemed too smart and savvy to fall for that kind of fashion faux pas."

"That is very strange. Anyone, really, could've walked into the grove. It's not like it's fenced off. And who made that call?" Concetta asked. "Do you think it was the owner?"

Audrey shrugged. "It didn't sound like him. And why would he call me there? I guess he might have, because he wanted someone to blame it on. He certainly didn't seem surprised by it."

Concetta shuddered. "How crazy. But don't worry, Dr. Smart. I am sure that the police are doing everything they can and will clear your name soon."

I don't know about that, Audrey thought. *The last few times, I had to do it myself.* "Until then," she said. "I can't leave town. It's standard procedure."

"Oh. Wow," Concetta said, as they heard the sound of the door in the reception area opening and closing. The women moved out to the front desk. Audrey expected the next patient. Instead, she saw Bambino's owner. The woman looked terrified.

Now there's the sight of a woman who will be devastated without her beloved pet, Audrey thought.

"Hello," she said kindly, approaching her. "It appears we're going to have to keep Bambino a little longer for—"

"No!" she shouted, taking a step back, and then another, into the corner like a frightened animal. She began to unleash the longest string of rambling Italian Audrey had ever heard, her voice high and frantic. The only word Audrey could make out was *Bambino.*

She looked at Concetta, whose eyes were wide. "What is she saying?"

"She's saying that she's come here to take Bambino with her, and she's not taking no for an answer."

51

"Can you tell her that Bambino is very sick and needs to stay a little—"

"She doesn't care. She's saying you can't keep her dog against her will."

"What? Why does she want to take Bambino away? He's not going to get better if--"

"She says she'd taking him into Palermo for a second opinion." Concetta stared at her as she ranted, pointing out the door like a madwoman. "She says that she heard what happened at the orange groves."

Already? How had that happened? She went to the computer and pulled up Bambino's owner's information. "*Scusi, Signora*—" She stopped when she saw the name on the card. "Ricci? Are you related to Officer Ricci?"

Concetta nodded. "Officer Ricci is her son."

"Oh, well, tell her I know her son, and that—"

She started to explode again with Italian, so fast that Audrey's head spun. Concetta shook her head, as if to say, *it doesn't matter. Nothing you will say matters.*

Audrey's face burned with indignation. Not only was that a bad sign on her clinic's part, it wasn't healthy for the dog. Moving him at this critical juncture wouldn't be wise. "Could you please tell Mrs. Ricci that it's extremely dangerous to move him right now?"

Concetta calmly explained to the woman, but the woman shook her head, her eyes fastened on Audrey, her mouth curved into a deep frown. "No."

Concetta said, "I'm sorry. Her mind's made up."

"But can you ask her why?" Audrey asked, her face flaming. She had never actually had a patient taken away from her. Well, often when she worked at the Back Bay Animal Hospital, people initially requested one of the other doctors in the practice, thinking because of her youthful appearance that she was an intern or technician who wasn't capable of handling the heavy issues. She'd usually been able to win them over, but still, having to work twice as hard as the male doctors to prove herself had been one of the more annoying aspects of her job. That wasn't supposed to happen in her own practice, where her name was on the door.

Concetta gently spoke to the woman, but it was clear from her tone of voice that it wasn't anything good. Concetta finally said, "She just wants a second opinion. And her decision is final."

Audrey frowned. *Is her decision because she already heard about the murder and my possible involvement in it?* She may have been a newcomer to Mussomeli, but she'd been there long enough to know that news—especially juicy gossip like that—travelled extremely fast around town. The streets were full of it.

"All right, right this way," she said, leading her into the back room.

She helped the woman get Bambino prepared for travel and watched sadly as the two left the clinic. Audrey knew she had no choice, but saving animals was her life, and this felt like a failure. There was only one thing she could think of that would fix things. And that was finding out who the true killer was, so that she could resume business as usual without her customers doubting her.

"Don't worry," Concetta said brightly after the woman had left, "Cheer up. It'll be okay. I'm sure the vet in Palermo will give her the same diagnosis."

"Yes," she murmured. "But I wanted to be the one to save him."

"You can't save every animal."

"But I can try," she whispered. *This time, I failed.*

"Hey," Concetta said, checking her phone. "You have your date tonight, right? With the American hunk?"

Audrey stared at her. The change of subject was so jarring that at first it didn't compute. Date? What date? American hunk? Who was that?

But suddenly, it came flooding back. She did have a date. With Mason.

And after everything she'd been through today, she felt like the walking dead. She shook her head. "I don't think it's a good idea that I go. Not with everything going on. Plus, I'm so tired. I should probably—"

"Nonsense! What better way to get your mind off it all?"

"Yes, but you've been at the clinic almost twenty-four hours straight, Concetta, and I'm not a slave-driver. I promised I'd relieve you when I got back from the grove, and now I—"

"Fine, relieve me," she said with a smile. "Now that Bambino is gone, we don't need to stay here twenty-four hours. All the other animals will be just fine overnight."

53

Audrey hesitated. She did have a point. But she wasn't sure if she wanted to do the suitor-juggling thing right now, after all that had happened. It felt like stirring a can of worms that she should just leave alone. "But—"

"Come on, Doctor," Concetta said, grabbing her jacket and keys and donning some fashionable sunglasses. "You need to go. That man has it bad for you. Don't break his beautiful heart."

With a wave, Audrey's vet intern stepped out the door.

Audrey stood there, rehashing the whole Bambino incident, and cringing. Yes, it would be nice to get her mind off things, and Mason, as an American, was probably the person she related to best.

I'll keep it a friendly get-together, she told herself to keep the pressure off. *Not a date.*

But she wasn't sure she could trust Mason to follow her lead. What if he only complicated things?

Groaning, she slid into the chair and sighed. *I'll cancel.*

Then she thought of his cute little dimple. And how her sister, Brina, seemed to think they were a match made in heaven.

Or not.

She buried her face in her hands and let out a long, agonized groan.

CHAPTER TEN

At seven that night, Mason rapped on the door.

Audrey felt like the dead. She'd showered, changing into a nice sundress, and put her hair into a bun, applying light lip gloss and mascara, hoping to get into the right, festive kind of mood. But it hadn't helped much. The bruise on her forehead was still terrible, she had about a thousand itchy mosquito bites from the orange grove, and yet those were the least of her problems.

It was too much to think about. But she was glad she hadn't cancelled on Mason, because she really didn't feel like being alone, either.

She opened the door to reveal her handsome neighbor from *via Milano*. He was freshly showered, his cinnamon hair a little wet, and carrying a picnic basket. Those ice-blue eyes settled on her and his perfect lips spread into a smirk, revealing those dimples and perfectly white teeth. He had the same effect on her as always—she started to smolder. She fought the urge to fan her face.

"Hi. What's that?" she said, pointing at the basket.

When he drawled, "How y'all doing, Boston?" it still managed to tug on her heartstrings, even with everything going on. The man was all about jeans and cowboy boots. She'd never seen him in anything else. "It's a surprise. What happened there?"

He was looking at her forehead. "Don't ask."

"Something with the house renovations? You know you could've asked me, if you needed the help."

Oh, she did. She probably would've, if he hadn't asked her on this date. But now, things felt strained. She didn't tell him that, though. Instead, she said, "I'm going to. At the end of the night. My faucet's leaking."

"Which one?"

"Kitchen."

"Didn't you just replace that?"

"Yes. But apparently I did it wrong."

He cocked his head to one side to look over her shoulder. His eyes always seemed to gleam with excitement whenever there was something that needed his magic wizard's touch. "I can——"

"No, no. Later!" Turning out the kitchen light, she looked over to his right and saw Polpetto, his giant adopted mastiff, wagging his tail excitedly. She leaned over to pet him. "Is this a pet-friendly evening?"

"Yep." He shrugged. "I figured you'd appreciate."

She smiled, patting her heart, touched. Jewels and flowers might be the way to the hearts of some women; animals had always been the way into hers. "I love it." She looked around. "But where's Nick?"

He motioned to a crack between her house and the one beside it. "Took one look at old Polp here and bolted."

Audrey sighed. Their pets had always had a rather tenuous relationship. "Oh well. I guess he'll catch up." She closed the door behind her and stepped off the stoop. "Lead the way."

They headed down toward the outside of town, which was great, since the last thing Audrey wanted to do was run into G. Or the police. Or, really, anyone, after the way that Bambino's owner had treated her. When they got to the steps that led down to the lake, he turned back to her. "You okay with this?"

"I'm fine. Thanks," she said, following him, even though she wasn't sure she would be able to climb up, later. The run up from the orange grove had been a killer. But she stepped after him, trying her best to be agreeable and enjoy it, since he'd clearly put a lot of thought into it. "Are we going to the lake?"

He nodded. "Best place to watch the sunset."

"Oh?" It made the hairs on the back of her neck stand on end. Not because she'd once found a body on the beach, a couple months ago. Not because it was a favorite place of poor strays who had no place to go.

It was because it sounded *romantic*. Really romantic. They'd be alone, watching the sunset . . . could anything spell romance more clearly?

As usual, the stone staircase to the beach was busy with people, coming back from their exercise and strolls around the gorgeous lake. Luckily, Audrey didn't happen upon her neighbor Nessa; this was her favorite running trail, and of course, if she'd heard the latest rumors, she'd be sure to get her digs in about how Audrey had been implicated in yet another murder.

Mason plucked the front of his t-shirt and sniffed. "Gee. Do I smell, or what?"

"What do you mean?" she asked nonchalantly, carefully watching her step as she took the steep stairs.

"Everyone's looking at me like they want to kill me."

"What?" She paused.

"Did you notice how people are looking at me?"

The first person she saw, a woman in a ponytail, glared at her. She took another step and noticed more, staring at her. Those whose eyes she caught seemed to scowl in disgust. Some of them stepped aside, as if they were afraid that she'd pull a gun on them. Did all the town already know?

"It's not you," she mumbled.

"Then who?" He laughed. "You? What'd you do now, Boston?"

"I'll tell you later."

They reached the bottom of the staircase and walked the long, tree-lined path to the clearing, where the sandy white beach spread out before them. Beyond that, the lake itself was like a mirror, reflecting the dying sun. It was like a postcard.

Polpetto rushed ahead, after a butterfly, like a giddy puppy, snapping his jaws in the air, trying to catch the thing. Mason stopped at the edge of the lake and pulled out a blanket, which he laid out on the sand. "So . . . how was your trip?"

She'd been staring out at the placid scenery, thinking how nature could seem so beautiful, even while a murder was taking place. Here. The orange grove. She shuddered. "Uh, what?"

"Your trip?" Confused, she still stared at him until he said, "I asked you if you needed anything yesterday and you told me you were going up to Montagna to see if you could find your dad? Did you?"

"Oh! Right." She barely remembered the conversation. She'd been vague about it to everyone, but Concetta and him. "No. Dead end."

"That's a shame." He motioned for her to sit.

She dropped to her knees, and he did, on the other side of the blanket. He opened the flap of the picnic basket, and immediately she smelled something delicious. He pulled out a big basket of fried chicken and biscuits. Delicious American food. The Colonel couldn't have done it better.

"You made this?"

He shrugged humbly. "You can take the kid out of the south, but you can't take the south out of the kid. I've been dying for good fried chicken since I landed my butt here. You like it?"

She nodded. Even though she hadn't had much appetite, up to now, she was surprised to find her mouth watering. "Absolutely."

He brought out a carton of fruit salad and spooned a little on a plate for her, then handed her a biscuit and drumstick. Then he poured two glasses of wine.

She peeled the crispy skin off the chicken and took a nibble of it. *Wow. This man knows how to cook.* "This is great."

Mason leaned back on his elbows, his legs stretched out and crossed in front of him, staring at the lake. "I know."

She wanted to smack him. There was that ego again. "Aren't you eating?"

"Yep. But I want to see what you think, first." Polpetto came bounding up, and he tossed him some meat off the drumstick, which the dog eagerly took. "All right, boy. Here you go, Polp."

She stared at the overflowing bucket. "I don't think the three of us can eat all this."

He shrugged as he sipped his wine. "We have all night."

Audrey yawned on cue, and her skin began to tickle like it'd been marred by a thousand mosquito bites. She scratched at it. "Probably not *all* night. I have to get back. I have all these bites . . ."

He reached into his pocket and pulled out some insect repellant, which he tossed to her.

"I didn't know you were a boy scout," she said, a little sourly, because now, all of her excuses to go home were gone.

He rolled over on his side and looked at her. "I didn't know you were in such a rush to get away from me."

"I'm not!" she protested. She looked down at her plate. Sure, she might not have felt that way, but that was probably how it *looked*. She couldn't blame him for thinking it. "I'm sorry. You're amazing. This was so nice. And . . ."

And I'm feeling guilty because my mind's not on the date, and because I'm going to have to let one of you go.

"It's not you. I promise you."

"Then what is it?"

"Just . . . a lot on my mind."

There was a silence, in which the only sound was that of the small waves, lapping at the shore.

"Not a problem. You want to talk about it?"

She didn't, really. She wanted to go back to her room, away from people who might accuse her with their eyes, and hole up in her bed. She stared at her wine. She didn't even have the appetite for that, after the earlier Prosecco. But when she looked up, he was staring at her, and his eyes were the first she'd seen in a long time that weren't accusing. They were sympathetic.

So, she said, "Those people were staring at me because they must think I'm a killer."

He let out a laugh. When she didn't laugh along with him, he said, "That murder of that councilwoman is water under the bridge. They can't possibly think you did it. The murderer was caught, remem—"

"There's been another murder," she said.

"Come on."

"It's true. Everyone in town knows about it. Why don't you? What rock were you hiding under?"

His eyes widened in astonishment. "I was under the house all day. Working on my crawl space. There was a murder? Who? Where?"

"In that orange grove outside of town."

"You mean that mafia place?"

At least he wasn't completely oblivious to the gossip. "Right."

"And what do you have to do with that?"

"I got a call that there was an injured animal out there, so I went to see if I could help. And instead—" She stopped, gauging how she wanted to tell the story. If she told him about that lunch with Rafael, would that qualify as a date? Would he be jealous? Better to steer away from that. "Instead, I found the body."

"So why would they think you had anything to do with it?"

"I don't know."

"I mean, the place is mafia. What do they expect to happen at places like that? Flower festivals?"

"No one knows for sure if it's mafia. The owner didn't really look the type. He seemed nice, not like a—"

"You met the owner?"

She nodded.

"You think everyone in the mafia looks like Marlon Brando?"

59

"No, but . . . I mean, maybe he was mafia. I don't know. The police questioned him, and I think he gave them the impression that I was the killer."

"Now why would they think that?"

"Because I was trespassing, and because he sneaked up on me and scared me, made me nervous. So I guess I just *look* guilty."

"But you're not. Anyone who knows you knows that," he said. "So I wouldn't worry."

She rolled her eyes. "You don't get it. If the mafia has the local police in their pocket, and is setting me up as their patsy, then it doesn't matter if I'm guilty. I'll go to jail."

He nodded thoughtfully. "But you said you don't know if he is mafia."

"I don't, but . . ."

"Seems to me that's the first thing you need to find out."

She put her drumstick down and took a sip of wine, then settled down on the blanket and tried to get comfortable. "I guess. I just wish that it wasn't me, finding all these dead bodies. It's no wonder the police are suspicious of me. Did I tell you I found one in Lipari?"

He nodded, and she remembered the conversation. It seemed like ages ago, even though it was just last week. With everything happening to her, it felt like she hadn't a second to catch her breath.

And she *definitely* didn't have the time to focus on picking a boyfriend. Even with a perfect one, staring her straight in the eye. How could she?

"That's some bad luck, Boston."

"I think I'm cursed." *And maybe, if I decide to date you more than casually, my bad luck will rub off on you.*

He tilted his head toward the moon, and his hair tousled in the breeze. "Nah. Look at it this way. You're here, in the most beautiful place on Earth."

She smiled. He was right; the sky was dazzling pink, dappling oranges and purples all over the placid lake, and all above them, stars were beginning to pop out. The beach's sand was warm and pleasant between her toes. It was quiet and calm, without another soul in sight, like one of those moments she wanted to bottle and keep, forever.

He continued, "With the most beautiful guy on Earth."

This time, she did reach over and smack him. As egotistical as he could be, she knew he was only kidding.

He chuckled and sat up, wiping his hands on his jeans to get rid of the sand. "Come on. You look tired. Eat up, and I'll take you home. What you probably need is a good night's sleep. Not all the excitement I can provide."

She shook her head. "But you went through all this trouble."

"Yeah. And I'll hold it against you at a later date, too. Eat."

She laughed and finished the food on her plate, as he told her a little bit about the renovations he'd been doing in his house. Contrary to Audrey's place, his was almost done, and now he was just putting on a number of finishing touches. He was building a massive dog house for Polpetto on the back patio, fit for a king. Funny, considering he used to say he didn't like pets. Now, he and Polpetto were inseparable.

When she was done, she finished her wine. "Strange. I was in such a bad mood. But now I actually feel better. So thank you."

"That's the Mason Magic," he teased, blowing on his fingernails and buffing them on his shirt front. "You're welcome."

"Oh, yes. I've heard it's legendary. I'm so blessed."

"Damn straight."

Nick appeared at the edge of the beach, carefully watching Polpetto, who let out a sharp bark.

"Quiet, boy," Mason said, snapping his fingers.

Audrey motioned Polpetto to her. She patted his side and turned back to Mason. "I'm sorry I wasn't very good company tonight. Maybe we'll do it again sometime, if you don't mind being with a cursed person?"

He nodded. "We will. And you ain't cursed. You're fine."

Then she thought of G, and her good mood dissolved. She didn't care what Concetta said about it being fine to date around. It simply felt wrong.

*

They were silent as Mason walked her back to her place.

She swallowed, and her voice a whisper, said, "Mason, I should probably tell you that—"

He held up a finger, pressing it against her lips. "It's all right. You don't have to tell me anything."

"But—"

"Go." He pointed forcefully to her door. "Besides, I already know. You think I'm great."

She burst out laughing. "No!" Then she blushed. "No, I mean, sure, you are, but you already know that, so I wasn't going to tell you it. What I was going to say is—"

"Girl. It's late. Let's not go into this now. Get some rest. I'll call you in the morning and see if I can come in and fix that faucet of yours, okay?"

"Thanks, Mason," she said, smiling gratefully at him before turning and heading inside. As she closed the door, she saw a red blur at her feet. Nick slipped in. She peered into the street and saw Mason sauntering away, one hand in the pocket of his jeans, like he hadn't a care in the world.

If only I could be that carefree, she thought.

"All right, Bub, I'll get you that apple," she said, replaying the date over again and again in her head. How sweet was he? Making her that picnic dinner so that they could eat it on the beach, together? Handy, funny, handsome and the total package. Among men, he was a complete gem. She should've been jumping on the opportunity to date him.

And she'd totally blown it. Bad timing, again.

Why did he like her, again? *Maybe I shouldn't worry about the murder and let the police sort it out.*

She cut the apple and rinsed it under the faucet, which was now leaking more than ever. Luckily, the bucket under the pipes was only filled about halfway. It could wait until Mason had a chance to look at it. Setting it down in Nick's tray, she turned and looked around her half-finished wreck of a house.

Since when did I NOT worry about things? It's in my nature. Besides, the police won't sort anything out if the mafia's involved. And I'll be the one left dangling.

Which reminded her, what Mason had said was true. She needed to find out what she was dealing with. Was Rafael Piccolo part of the mafia?

Tomorrow, she decided, she would go and find out. Somehow.

CHAPTER ELEVEN

Audrey rolled over in bed and felt a weight on her chest.

The weight of the police, bearing down on her? The mafia, wanting a piece of her? The men in her life, wanting her to make a decision?

No.

Feeling breathless, she cracked open an eyelid. It was the weight of Nick, sitting right on her mid-section. Again.

"Ugh. Could you please try to not crush me so early in the morning, every morning?" she groused, shooing him away. He scampered off, to the open picture window, and climbed out onto the ledge. Little ninja that he was, she didn't think her rejection was enough to get him to commit suicide, but she still scrambled from the bed and poked her head out, just to be sure.

Sure enough, he was perched on the narrow road outside her house, licking his paws and watching as neighbor Nessa, from across the street, approached, a cameraman in front of her, capturing her every move. She was wearing her jogging clothes and carrying a to-go coffee container, saying, in a sweet voice that Audrey didn't recognize, "Yes, after my morning 5K, I usually stop by at the local coffee shop around the corner for my espresso. It's part of my morning routine and keeps me awake so I can handle another busy day of renovations. Today, I'm going to show you how to make your bathroom . . ."

Suddenly, there was a sharp squeal and a "What the . . ." Audrey looked over just as Nick disentangled himself from the cameraman's legs. Unfortunately, it wasn't soon enough, because the man stumbled backwards, landing on his backside. His camera went skidding across the street.

Audrey winced.

Nessa, scowling, snapped her glare up to Audrey. "Hello? We're filming here! Could you please keep that mongrel of yours out of the way, murderer!"

Audrey rolled her eyes. Now *that* was the Nessa she knew and couldn't stand. "Sorry."

She went downstairs to berate Nick, but by the time she got there, he'd already disappeared. Nessa was standing there, hands on hips, talking with the cameraman as she looked at his footage. "I think we need to do another take completely. My nose looks shiny."

"Well, you were supposed to have gotten back from a run?" he suggested gently.

"So?" She looked around. "Makeup! Where is makeup?"

Her eyes landed on Audrey. "So I heard you murdered a mafia guy, now," she said with a smile. "You know, Audrey, if you're trying to become a serial killer, you might want to pick your victims more wisely."

"Ha," Audrey said.

"Seriously, though. What were you doing there?"

Audrey's first instinct was to slam the door and not give Nessa any more of her time. But she decided to humor her. "I got an anonymous call about an injured animal in the orange groves."

"Right. Likely story. Didn't you get one of those the last time?"

This time, she actually did slam the door on her. She knew nothing she could say would appease Nessa. In fact, the first time she'd met Nessa, the woman had done everything in her power to get Audrey arrested for a murder. Despite Audrey's attempts to smooth things over, it had only gone downhill. To say they weren't friendly was an understatement; now, Audrey didn't even bother to try.

Besides, she had better things to do than to get accused by Nessa. As she went into the shower to get ready for the day, she thought about the man who'd been murdered. The name clearly hadn't rung a bell with the police, so he was likely a stranger, unknown to anyone in the area. His dress—the dark suit—seemed wildly out of place for a country town. So why had he come to Mussomeli? What was his purpose? Why would he be traipsing about some orange grove in the mid-day?

Well, why had *she* been? She'd been called there. Maybe he had been, too.

The police had a flimsy motive for her . . . that she'd just been surprised and pulled a gun? Who would do that? So probably, likely, even if she did manage to get arrested, they wouldn't have enough evidence. But something told Audrey there was a different reason that they were focusing so hard on her, and practically ignoring Rafael Piccolo, the owner of the estate.

Mafia?

Right. That was the big question. And she needed to find out.

When she climbed out of the shower and put on a robe, throwing her hair in a towel turban, she climbed upstairs to her room and got out her phone. She quickly typed in: *Rafael Piccolo.*

There were plenty of hits, so she added the word: *Palermo.*

That gave her more targeted results. There was plenty of old information about some Piccolo family that had possible mob ties, but nothing very recent. She clicked on one article and read:

Sicilians are breathing a sigh of relief that Cosa Nostra's grip on Palermo is now over. The police have, in recent years, arrested over 4,000 individuals with known ties to the criminal family. Between 1978 and 1983, the Sicilian mafia, notably the Piccolo clan, killed more than 1,000 people. Hundreds were murdered in the early '80s. Since the mid-1990s, the number of homicides has decreased significantly. The last five years in Palermo have seen only one homicide attributable to Cosa Nostra. For those who have lived in fear of retaliation by this powerful family, it is a breath of fresh air. But some warn that the mafia's roots run too deep to ever be fully extracted . . .

Audrey shuddered. Though it was great that they were no longer powerful in Palermo, that didn't mean that they wouldn't find other places to do business. *Lie low,* which was what Piccolo had told her.

And what if that's exactly what he was doing? What if he had killed that man, then set about framing her for the murder? Maybe that was why he invited her to lunch . . . to get her fingerprints from her wine glass, which he could plant on the body? She wasn't quite sure *how* he'd do such a thing, but *he* was the criminal mastermind. That might have been his entire family's life's work. There might have been a very good reason that he'd invited her to lunch with him, which had nothing to do with the fish.

She checked her watch. It was just eight o'clock. She had time to go down to the orange grove and look around prior to opening the clinic for her first appointment at ten.

Dressing quickly, she headed out, doing her best to avoid the camera crews who'd taken up residence outside her house. Luckily, they weren't there for her . . . yet.

*

65

Audrey made it down to the grove within minutes, with Nick trailing close behind. Despite how sunny and cheerful the grove was, with its big not-quite-ripe oranges, dotting the trees in the sun, it was eerie, walking around a place where a murder had been committed. She sucked in her breath and walked among the trees, trying to find the place where the body had lain.

She arrived there a few moments later—or at least, she thought it was the right place. There was no crime scene tape, no outline of the body, nothing that one would see on murder mysteries. In fact, there was nothing to show a crime had been committed there at all. It seemed as though the police had concluded their investigations and found everything they needed to.

But had they found the gun? Or anything else?

To Audrey, it seemed premature. Like they weren't even *trying*.

Or maybe something, or someone, was stopping them.

She walked around the place where the body had sprawled, moving the grass around with her toe. She wasn't sure what she was looking for, but whatever it was, she didn't find it. *Maybe they did do everything they could.*

Then she walked around the trees, peering in knots, staring at the ground, trying to find anything of interest. But the place was as clean as could be.

As she was looking around, Nick poked his head up, an orange in his paws. He started to munch on it while he watched her. "You go ahead," she said to him. "Have your breakfast while I look for clues."

He did exactly that.

"You could give me a little help," she complained. "You have that awesome nose of yours. I have nothing."

He continued to eat.

"All right, thanks for your support," she said, turning to walk in the other direction. As she did, she realized how close to the house she was. It was right in front of her, rising up from the trees. *I'd better get away from the house before the owner notices me and tells the police that I'm here. It could incriminate me. The murderer always returns to the scene of the crime, after all.*

No sooner had she started to back away when she heard the sound of footsteps, up ahead.

66

Before she could even think to hide behind one of the trees, Rafael Piccolo appeared, hands in pockets, as if he hadn't a care in the world. He caught sight of her and smirked. "Couldn't keep away, eh?"

Her heart caught. *Come on, Audrey, think of a good excuse.* But nothing came. It was his effect on her—that hypnotizing look in his brown eyes that made her weak. She was left with the truth. "I wanted to see if I could find clues as to who could've done that terrible thing."

"The murder?"

She stared at him. What other terrible thing was there? "Yes."

He nodded. "It was terrible. I agree. But I think the police might be able to take care of it, don't you?"

Audrey's starstruck nervousness from before faded away, and she remembered just what he'd said to the police. "If I let them have their way, they'd arrest *me*, thanks to you."

"Thanks to . . ." His eyebrows raised in shock. "What do you mean?"

She gave him an incredulous look. "How could you not know? You told them that I trespassed, I looked suspicious, that I was flustered, and that I'd been coming from where the body was found. So—"

"But all that was true," he said calmly.

"Yeah, well, maybe, but you didn't have to—"

"I didn't have to tell the truth to the police?" He seemed amused by this suggestion.

"No, of course you do, but did you have to make it seem like I was the killer?"

He held up his hands in surrender. "Well. I see. But to tell you the truth, I don't know you. I don't know for sure that you're not the killer."

She stood there, speechless.

He rubbed his chin as he looked her over. "But I suppose I should give you the benefit of the doubt. You don't look very much like a killer. Then again, I'm not quite sure if there is a typical killer 'look.'"

"*You* could be the killer," Audrey blurted.

He chuckled. "And why would you think that?"

"Well. It's your place. And you seemed entirely too calm when you found out a man had been murdered here."

"Did I?"

"Yes. You didn't look shocked, you didn't ask, *Who is it?* or *What happened?* You didn't seem to care at all. It seemed like you already knew Pietro Grinnelli, and you were happy he was dead."

"Pietro . . . ?"

"Grinnelli."

He shook his head. "Sorry. It doesn't ring a bell."

Her ears burned. Either he was doing a good job pretending, or he really never had heard the man's name before. "I still find your actions suspicious. But the police didn't. In fact, the police didn't find a lot of what you said or did suspicious. It made me wonder what, exactly, you talked about."

"What do you mean?"

"I mean, whether you, I don't know . . ." She looked up, trying to think of the best way to phrase *Used your mafia brawn to intimidate them.* "Er . . .exerted certain power . . ."

He laughed. "Power? I'm sure I don't know what you mean."

She blew out a breath of air. "Your reaction was odd, is all. And the police didn't seem to question you on it."

"On the contrary. They *did* question me on it. And I suppose I passed with flying colors. I guess I don't find dead people something to get hysterical over. And I didn't think I would know the man—I don't know anyone around here," he explained. "But I guess I'm jaded. There's quite a lot of crime in Palermo."

"Is there? But so close to home? On your property?"

His eyes narrowed. "Dr. Smart, what exactly are you implying?"

She sighed. All this beating around the bush was exhausting. Taking a deep breath, she decided to just come out with it. She blurted, "Are you mafia?"

She expected his eyes to widen in surprise, but they didn't. It was as if he was used to being asked the question.

"No, of course not. That's ridiculous."

"There have been rumors . . ."

"Yes. I suppose there are," he said, nodding. "There always are, in towns like these. But again, whoever's been talking is mistaken."

She nodded, relieved. "And you really have no idea who the murdered man is?" she asked, watching him carefully to see if he gave anything away.

But either he was a very practiced liar, or he was innocent. And really, he didn't look like mafia at all. "None at all. But I suppose that

68

puts us both in a bad position, since you and I were the only ones in the grove."

"Not necessarily," she said, to his surprise. She laughed a little. "I'm sorry. I was up all night, thinking about it. And my thought is that . . . well, what about your servants?"

"Servants?" He chuckled. "I only have one. Marta. She's been with my family since I was a boy. And even if she was the type to go around shooting people, I don't exactly give her much time to engage in such pursuits. Taking care of my needs is a round-the-clock endeavor."

"Oh." That kind of ruled out most of her thoughts. "I saw someone else, in the grove, though."

"Someone else?"

"Yes. I think the person was wearing a hat, white, with red polka dots. Or it might have been a scarf."

"Scarf? In this heat?"

"That's why I'm leaning toward hat. Or something."

He shrugged. "I can't say I'm fond of polka dots."

She smiled. That's what Concetta had said. "I didn't think so. I—" She froze. Concetta. The clinic. She scrabbled for her phone and checked the display. It was almost ten o'clock. "Oh, no! I've got to go. I have an appointment at the clinic in fifteen minutes!"

She started to rush off, but he called, "Dr. Smart. I hope I'll see you again? Perhaps for dinner?"

"Uh. Sure," she said, backing away. "But why don't we hold off on that until after I find out who killed Pietro Grinnelli?"

"*You* are going to find out?" He sounded doubtful.

"Don't worry. I've done it before," she called as she left, and then wondered, all the way back to the clinic, if she should've said such a thing. If he'd been lying to her, if he really *was* mafia and had killed that man, the last thing he probably wanted around was a snoop who could spoil his whole operation.

She didn't need that to worry about, now. Her day was full of appointments.

But it didn't matter. She couldn't help feeling, the closer she got to the clinic, that she'd painted a target, right on her own back.

CHAPTER TWELVE

It was after two when Audrey finished up with her appointments for the day. Exhausted she slumped into the chair at the reception desk and fired off a bill to the last customer, then clutched her growling stomach. *Why are you acting like this, stomach? Was it something I ate? Stop!*

She checked her appointments for the following day, thinking about her conversation with Rafael. Now, she felt a little better that he wasn't from the mob . . . but she wasn't one-hundred-percent on that. Her gut told her that no, he wasn't a cold-blooded killer. She hoped.

So that left the person with the polka dots.

Which wasn't helpful. She'd never seen anyone wearing polka dots, anywhere in town.

And really, who were either of them to recognize that person? She and Rafael were both outsiders. What she needed was someone who knew this town and its inhabitants, inside and out . . .

Light bulb. She needed G.

Suddenly, the growling in her gut became so loud, it practically drowned out her own thoughts.

After a minute, she realized the reason: *Oh. I haven't eaten anything all day.*

Another light bulb. She needed to get to *La Mela Verde,* right away.

At that, her stomach let out a sharp, piercing cry, like, *Finally she gets the picture.*

"Concetta!" she called into the back room as she gathered her purse. "I'm going to get something to eat. Want to come?"

No answer.

It was only when she wandered into the back room that she remembered she'd given Concetta the day off. *I'm totally losing it. I need a meal. Sleep. Time to think.*

She decided to close up shop for an hour and get something to eat at *La Mela Verde.* At least there, she'd meet one friendly face and pick his brain for a nice, quiet lunch.

As she walked through the town, she tried not to dwell on the fact that she might be a mob target. There were boys playing a card game on a front stoop of a house, and people sitting out, enjoying the warm weather in the *piazza*. No one seemed to be looking at her suspiciously, which was a good thing. Even so, she couldn't help looking over her shoulder, expecting some man with a machine gun to emerge from a dark alley and shoot her dead.

You've got to get a grip, Audrey, she thought, even as she picked up the pace and crossed the street.

As she passed her home, she noticed something.

Her heart crammed itself in her throat as she neared the door.

Yes, she wasn't imagining it. There was a note, the size of a large post-it, attached to it.

She crept closer, cringing at the thought of opening it to find a mob love-letter: *You're next!* scrawled in blood.

But instead, she could see rather neat, boxy handwriting, that looked rather familiar: *Stopped in to fix that leak but you were out. Tonight?-- M*

Mason. Oh. Right.

Her momentary relief gave way to panic as she realized she hadn't emptied the bucket since last night. She rushed inside, sloshing through a quarter-inch puddle of water that was stretching out over the kitchen floor.

"Oh, no no no!" she shouted, opening the cabinet door. Sure enough, the bucket was full. She grabbed it, took it over to the front door, and emptied it.

Stuffing it back under the cabinet, she growled to herself. Her tile floor would likely be fine, but the throw rug she had by the kitchen table was drenched. She grabbed a broom and half-heartedly started to sweep the water out the front door. Then she sighed. *I can't deal with this right now.*

Throwing the broom down, she locked up her house and went on her way. She was halfway up the street, within a block of the café, when she heard a commotion, two male voices, raised in anger.

Great. What now?

One of the men was wearing an apron and a flat-topped hat, standing in front of a street cart that sold gelato. Audrey had bought some from him, several times, and he'd always been very pleasant. But now, his face was red, and he was gesticulating wildly. The other man, a bearded, large bear of a man, was doing the same. It was like they

71

were having a shouting match, but since they were speaking Italian, Audrey had no idea what they were saying.

People were starting to gather around, watching the spectacle. Audrey didn't have time for that. Her stomach was begging for food, and unfortunately, these men were in her path.

As she broke through, intending to go past them, the bear of a man clenched his fist. Were they really going to come to blows?

Audrey couldn't ignore it anymore. She said, "What seems to be the problem?"

The bear man looked at her, relief on his face. "You speak English?"

She nodded. "I'm American. What's going on?"

"I'm from the mainland. I just asked this man where I can get some real food, and he starts yelling at me. *This is real food,* or something. All I want to do is sit down somewhere and get a nice meal. I no understand these Sicilians."

"Ohhh," Audrey said. She'd long since heard the distaste that Sicilians and mainland Italians had for one another, but she'd never seen it in action. "I understand. I'm actually heading to the best café in Mussomeli right now. You can follow me, if you'd like."

He sighed, clearly happy by the invitation. "I'd love that. Thank you."

Audrey smiled at the food cart man and patted his arm. "It's all right," she said, smiling. "I will take care of him."

He let out a grunt and started to wheel his cart away, and the crowd began to disperse.

As Audrey walked with the man, she realized how large he was. From the gray in his sideburns, she gathered he was probably about sixty, but he hadn't yet gotten smaller or frailer in the way some older men did. He was built like a linebacker. She barely reached his shoulder, and he was as wide and round as a barrel. *That food cart guy had a lot of guts, yelling at him. He looks like he could've killed him in two seconds flat.*

Determined not to get on his bad side, she said, "So, what brings you to Mussomeli?"

"Passing through," he said shortly. "Why are you in the area?"

"I bought one of those one-dollar houses on a whim. So I'm fixing it up."

"Is that so? I've heard of that. I'd be interested in that. What is the area like?"

"Oh, it's really nice. Nice, small town feel. People are very friendly," she said, and almost as if to prove it, a woman she'd seen a couple times before waved at her. She waved back.

"Is there a lot of crime?"

"Crime? Oh, no. Not at—" She stopped. "Well, to be truthful, there was a murder here yesterday. Someone was shot in the back. Outside of town. But that was probably just an odd occurrence." *I probably shouldn't talk of the other two murders. I'd scare him away for good.*

"Odd occurrence? You mean, they don't know who did it?"

"No. The police are looking into it. It's a small town, so I'm sure they'll probably find out who it was, soon." *Though they might need my help.*

"There's a criminal element in this town?"

"Well, there is talk that it might have something to do with the mob."

"The mob?" Now, he seemed really interested. "I did not know *Cosa Nostra* reached this far inland. That's fascinating, their power. I thought they were all but dead."

"They probably are. Honestly, I wouldn't believe any of the talk you hear around here. This town gossips about anything and everything. The thing is, it's very safe to walk these streets, even at night. It never bothered me at all. This place gets very quiet after sundown," she said with a smile. "So if you are thinking of buying and bringing your family here, I wouldn't hesitate."

He nodded. "I suppose I'd need to find the right property."

They'd reached the end of the road, and the sign for *La Mela Verde* came into view. She pointed to it. "Well, this is it. Prepare to be dazzled. G makes some of the best food in town. If I were you, I'd have his *arancini.*"

He smiled. "I'm grateful. What's your name?"

"Audrey. I'm Audrey Smart. I'm the town veterinarian. My clinic's on *Barcellona*." She extended her hand.

He shook it. "Marco. Good to meet you."

"Likewise! Have a good lunch."

He held the door open for her as she walked into the busy café. Right now, she had to seek out G. She had some questions to ask him.

73

CHAPTER THIRTEEN

"*Principessa!*" G shouted across the busy café as she approached, his voice so loud that it drowned out all the other noises. "Finally, I see you again!"

Once again, *La Mela Verde* was busy, full of expats and locals alike, all enjoying the cozy atmosphere. The place was decorated in grape vines, with wine casks everywhere, and most of the tables were small and packed close together, to make the most of the limited space. Everyone, of course, was smiling, because that was the effect G's food had on a person—it simply was impossible to be in a bad mood after eating his delicacies.

She smiled as she stepped up to the counter, happy to see that her spot, at the end of the bar, was open. She slid onto the stool. "*Ciao.*"

He passed a glass of water over to her. "So what is going on in the good doctor's world? It is like I have not seen you in ages!"

What hasn't been going on, is the real question, she thought, taking a sip of the water. "I've been dying for your *ciambotta.* Please."

"Ah, it's been one of those kinds of days, eh?" he said, scooping some of the golden stew out of a giant vat and handing it to her, with a hunk of crusty bread.

"One of those *lives.*" She smiled. "What else is new?"

He laughed and leaned up against the counter. New customers arrived, and he motioned to one of the waitresses to take care of it. "You Americans do live exciting lives, no?"

"I don't know about that. It's only since I moved here that my life has been crazy. In Boston, I was boring," she said, scooping some of the vegetable stew into her spoon and bringing it to her lips, pausing a moment to inhale. This was, by far, her favorite food of all the new flavors she'd sampled since coming to Sicily. Warm, delicious, and simple, it was like a big bowl of mac n' cheese, at home. The best kind of comfort food.

And she *really* needed the comfort right now.

She tasted it and smiled. "Mmmm. So good. I needed that." She smacked her lips.

He chuckled. "So what's been on your mind? Something with the clinic?"

"No. Not really. You know that murder?"

He nodded. Of course, he'd be familiar with it. There was no gossip that spread through this town without G catching wind of it. He gave her a curious look. "Don't tell me . . ."

"Yes. I found the body. Again."

He stared at her in astonishment. Then he burst out laughing and slammed his palm into the counter. "I'm sorry. I don't mean to make light. But that is a very odd thing. We had almost no murders before you came here. And since then, three."

"And I found all three of them. I know, I know." She slumped over the bowl and scooped more into her mouth.

"How did you stumble upon this one?"

"It's weird. I got an anonymous call about an injured animal, down by the orange groves. I went there and found the body. He'd been shot in the back."

"The orange groves. You mean, Tivoli?" When she nodded, he said, "That was the place we were just talking about. The subject of all the mafia rumors."

"Right. I know you said it was ridiculous, but a dead guy being found there . . . shot in the back . . . it almost makes it seem true."

"Did you see the owner?"

She nodded, looking away. *I had lunch with the owner, but I'm not telling G that.* "He doesn't seem like a cold-blooded killer."

"Ah. Well, I'm sure the police will find out who did it."

"I don't know about that. Dinardo seems to think I did it."

G laughed again, pounding the counter so hard this time that the silverware rattled. "He can't."

"He does. I think. I don't know. They don't have any other suspects. And—" She looked around carefully to make sure no one was listening and then added, "At first I thought Rafael was mafia, and possibly paying them off to suspect me. But now, I don't know."

"Rafael?"

"Yes. Rafael Piccolo."

"Piccolo?" G's tan face went ashen. He stroked his chin. "That was an old clan family. But they've been gone for a while."

"But maybe their roots go deep," she whispered, repeating the article she'd read.

He shook his head. "I know Dinardo. He's a good man. He can't be bought. He will find the killer."

"I hope so." She finished her ciambotta and placed the spoon down. "That was one thing I wanted to ask you. Do you happen to know anyone who wears a white scarf or hat with red polka dots?"

His eyes danced with amusement. "Is this the clue to solving the whole mystery?"

"Possibly. I could've sworn I saw someone out in the grove, wearing that, right before the murder. But before I could get a closer look, the person was gone."

G crossed his arms, thinking. "Come to think of it, I do. Ugo. Ugo Telemaco. He's kind of a crazy old man. Lives not far from the grove, in fact, in a shack, next door. Keeps to himself. But he wears a hat like that." He made a face. "You might not want to go there, though. He's not the friendliest of men."

Ooh, that sounded like a lead. Here, she'd thought the convivial G didn't have an enemy on the whole island. "Not the friendliest of men? What does that mean?"

He shrugged. "There's a reason he lives outside of town. He likes his privacy. But you'll see, because I know you. No amount of my warning you away will do any good. You're going to go there, anyway. Right?"

She gave him an innocent shrug. "Well . . .when I get curious about something, I get an itch. And I can't stop until it's been scratched."

He reached under the counter and pulled out a cup of his famous pistachio gelato. "On the house."

"Thank you," she said, grabbing a dessert spoon and digging in. She was still hungry. "You definitely know the way to this girl's heart."

He leaned on the counter, closer to her. "Which reminds me. Friday night was fun. When do we do it again?"

She froze. Looked away. And here, she'd almost gotten off without a scratch.

"Oh. Um. Soon," she said, licking her spoon, then grabbing her purse and pulling out a few euros. She set down the money and slipped off the stool. "But I forgot. I have something back at the clinic to do. Thanks for the meal. We'll talk later?"

They said their goodbyes and she went outside, muttering to herself. Why had she mentioned the way to her heart? Like she even knew what her heart wanted, now, with everything going on.

Right now, she had one thing on her mind, and that was meeting Ugo Telemaco, the man with the polka-dotted hat. She had to find out why he was there, in the orange grove, at the time of the murder.

*

Audrey's legs ached as she took the steps for the second time that day, down to the grove. She knew it would only be worse, coming up, but that the trip would be worth it.

She'd only hoped to close the clinic for an hour. She was blowing that out of the water. But she didn't have any appointments, and the animals would be okay for a little longer. She had to know.

But when she arrived at the path that ran adjacent to the orange grove, she didn't know which way to turn. All she could see were orange trees, in all directions. Because she'd gone right, before, and that had led her around to the mansion, she took a left. The path gradually narrowed more and more until it was just a thin passage of trampled grass, into a heavily wooded area.

When she emerged from it, she saw the rusted metal roof, nearly invisible under a thick covering of vines. Walking closer, she saw a shack with a single window, shade drawn tightly.

Now here is someone who definitely does not want to be found. Too bad. I have to know why he was out there.

She paused there, thinking.

If he is the murderer, he really won't want to be found. Not only that, he'll probably have a gun.

Wiping her sweaty palms on her hands, she moved a bit further, until the pathway forked in two. One trail led off in the direction of the shack. She took it, trying to decide exactly what she'd say when she approached the man. The path wound around the shack, giving her a good idea of its size. It was little larger than an outhouse of old, on the prairie, and looked about as well-kept as one, too. At least it didn't smell like one—it smelled like the forest around it, like earth and decay and flora.

The front door was just three planks of wood, nailed together—completely windowless, as if its owner was perfectly content to shut away the outside world. She could only imagine how dark it was inside.

Audrey went up and, taking a deep breath, rapped sharply.

The door opened to reveal a man with a gray, unruly beard, in a white ribbed undershirt. He squinted at her, his eyes obviously unused to the sunlight.

"Hello, Mr. Telemaco?" she asked brightly. "I'm Audrey Smart, a veterinarian in town. Do you speak English? *Lei parla inglese?*"

He stared at her. "Huh?"

I guess that's a no. Audrey had been getting better with her Italian, but she was still lagging woefully behind. It hadn't helped her much, having Concetta to rely on at the clinic. Usually, she just looked at her assistant for help with translations. *I wish Concetta was here.* "I'm a doctor. *Dottore?*"

He stared at her. "*Dottore? No. No necessità.*" He went to close the door.

"No!" She shoved her hand in the way before he could. Pain ripped up her forearm as the door bounced off her elbow. He stared at her in surprise as she rubbed it. "Sorry. But I—"

"Oh, leave an old man be, would you? Can't you see I want to be left alone?" He groused, in perfect English.

Her eyes widened. "Oh. So you can speak English."

He looked up at the ceiling. "Yes. But I don't want to. Especially to a woman who's been trespassing on my grounds."

"If I'm not mistaken, you were the one trespassing on the grounds of the Tivoli estate, yesterday."

His eyes bulged, and he choked. "No, I wasn't."

"I saw you there. Running through the grove. Don't deny it."

He shook his head and pointed to his leg. It was only then that Audrey realized it was nothing more than a peg, like that of a pirate. "I can easily deny it. I don't run anywhere, anymore."

"Okay, so maybe not running, but *hobbling*. Quickly."

He shrugged. "All right. So what business is it of yours? Are you the new owner?"

"No. But a man was found murdered there, and you were seen there. So naturally I'm curious."

"Murdered?" he said, his voice not more than a whisper. "Are you sure?"

"Shot in the back."

"Shot?" He stared significantly at nothing, his eyes narrowing as if some important though had come to him.

"I'm surprised the police haven't been here to question you about it, considering your property backs up to the grove."

He looked around, agitated. "Well, they can't have thought I did it! Just because I was there? I had my reasons, and I promise you, it has nothing to do with murder."

"What were you doing there, then?"

"I was . . ." He scowled. "What difference does it make to you? You're not police. I have no obligation to tell you anything."

"True. But I'll be sure to let Detective Dinardo know what I saw so that he can question you."

"You wouldn't do that."

She shrugged. "Maybe. Look, if you tell me why you were there, maybe I won't tell them."

He sighed. "All right. All right. I was walking through the grove, picking up the oranges that fell on my property."

"On your property?"

He nodded. "It's not stealing. They should keep the limbs on their side. The ones on my side? Those are my oranges."

"But I thought I saw you on their property?"

He shook his head. "You can't prove it."

She realized he was right. She couldn't prove it. She had no idea where the property line was, and maybe it was true that he hadn't trespassed. Maybe when she'd seen him, he'd been on his side of the property.

The body, though? That had definitely been in the center of the grove, on the Tivoli estate. "Fine. Did you happen to hear or see anything while you were out, on *your* side of the property?"

He nodded. "I heard gunshots. A quick, one-two. *Bang-bang!*" He shouted in a loud voice that echoed through the grove, almost frightening her off his front stoop. "For a second, I thought someone was shooting at me. So I ran for it. I hid."

"I thought you said you couldn't run?" she pointed out, suspicious.

"Fine. I *hobbled* for it, if you want to split hairs," he snapped. "But then I heard nothing. So I went out to see if I could find out who was shooting at me, so I could give them a piece of my mind. *It was my property! My oranges!*" He scratched his grizzled jaw. "Where was the body found?"

"In the grove. Close to the house. It's a wonder you didn't stumble upon it."

"Not really. The grove is enormous. I didn't go near the house. Halfway there, I decided that if a man with a gun was the new owner, I probably shouldn't go there unarmed," he said, reaching behind him and pulling out a silver revolver, like something out of a wild west movie.

Audrey took a step backwards. Even though he wasn't pointing it at her, her body tensed. She wasn't sure what kind of gun had killed Pietro Grinnelli, but it didn't matter. Any gun was enough cause for concern.

"Ah, don't worry. It's not loaded." He seemed amused by her fear.

"Did you go back with the gun?" She couldn't tear her eyes away from it.

He shook his head. "Nope. I got lost in the grove. It took a while to find my way back. By the time I did, I decided it wasn't worth my trouble. So I sat down, had an orange, and took a nap." He gnawed on the inside of his cheek. "That was at around noon."

"Did you see anyone while you were there, in the grove?"

He nodded. "A girl in shorts. Dark hair. Standing on a rock. I think that might have been you?"

She nodded. That sounded about right, from her recollection.

"After that, I got out of there."

Audrey sighed. She believed him, even though he was carrying the very sort of weapon used to kill Pietro, because his story checked out. And why would he kill a person, and then stick around to steal oranges? If he'd known what happened, or been responsible for it, he likely would've denied he'd been there at all.

Because he was still holding the gun, much too casually than she would've liked, she backed away slowly. "All right. Well—"

"You're not going to tell the police what I told you, are you?" he asked.

"No, but they might find out themselves. You might want to save them the trouble and tell them, before they come looking for you."

"Bah, let them come. I got nothing to hide," he said, waving his hand at her. It was the one holding the gun. She'd read enough about gun misfires and accidental shootings to be more than a little afraid. She wasn't going to be the first one to turn her back on him; that was for sure. "*My* oranges."

"All right, well—"

"What's that?" His eyes caught on something off to her side, behind her. To her shock, he lifted the gun and slowly pointed it.

She looked over her shoulder just in time to see Nick, poking his head through the shrubbery. Fear gripped her. "No, that's my—"

"Dinner!" he said, as the gunshot went off.

Horrified, she watched as Nick yelped and ducked into the bushes.

"Idiot! That was my pet fox, Nick!" she growled, rushing off after him.

"Let me know if I got him!" he called, howling with laughter. "I've got a recipe for meat stew I want to try, and I was just missing the meat!"

Oh, no, she thought, shoving aside prickly tree limbs as she barreled into the bushes. *If anything happened to him, I'll never forgive myself. This is my fault for sticking my nose in business where it doesn't belong.*

"Nick! Are you okay?" she called, cupping her hands around her mouth, her heart racing like a runaway train. "Nick! Please! Answer me."

Tromping over the uneven ground between the two properties, she came to the first row of orange trees, which must've been the delineation line. No Nick. The poor thing must've run off, scared to death. Her brave little soldier, the creature who'd saved her numerous times. She couldn't believe this was happening.

She took a few more steps, sinking deeper and deeper into misery, when she saw it.

Droplets of bright red blood, on the grass.

"Oh," she murmured, tears flooding her eyes. He needed medical attention, as soon as possible. Straightening, desperate, she shouted louder than ever, "Nick!"

CHAPTER FOURTEEN

Audrey ducked under the branch of an orange tree, growing more and more frightened. She called to the little fox again, but all she heard on the breeze was her own voice, echoing back to her.

"Oh no," she said aloud as she meandered deeper into the grove, looking for any sign. But there were no footprints, no blood stains other than the first one she'd seen. He'd likely vanished, afraid. Leave it to that jerk Ugo to destroy his faith in the human race. Maybe she'd never see him again.

Her heart lurched at the thought. Though she hadn't planned on having a fox as a pet, he'd followed her around those first few days, endearing himself to her. Over the months, she'd gotten quite attached to him. "This is what I get for being too curious. I put those I love in danger. Nick!"

Just when she was about to give up, she heard it: A slight whimper, coming from the bushes.

She rushed over to them and found him, curled in a ball and mewling softly.

"Oh, Nick," she said, her heart breaking for him. She moved forward, but he flinched. "Don't worry. I'm not going to hurt you."

This time, he let her move aside his bushy tail so she could assess the damage. One of his little legs had a spot of blood; maybe it had been grazed by the bullet, but it didn't seem to be any worse than how he'd been the first day she'd found him, caught in Mason's fence. Other than that little spot, he seemed to be intact. She sighed with relief. "Oh, thank goodness! I think you'll be okay." She wiped her sweaty palms on her shorts. "But we've got to get back to the clinic and patch that up. Come on."

She lifted him into her arms, cradling his injured leg. The poor little guy was trembling. She held him to her body to keep him safe and hurried the entire way to town. Though she'd be dreading the walk back up, she barely noticed it, so concerned was she with Nick. When she got back to the clinic, the door was already open.

83

She rushed inside to find Concetta, doing paperwork at the reception desk. "What are you doing here?" she asked in shock. "I thought I gave you the day off?"

"Yes, but I had so much work to catch up on. Goodness. What happened?" she asked, jumping to her feet.

Audrey looked down as she headed to surgery, still holding Nick tight. His heart was beating so fast she thought it might give out. Her white shirt was now had a couple drops of blood on it, making the injury look worse than it was. "Some crazy guy outside of town thought he'd make Nick his dinner."

Concetta followed her into the room as she laid Nick down and looked around for a sedative to relax him. "Dinner? Really? Gross."

Audrey shrugged as she found the vial and filled the syringe. *Sweet dreams, Bub,* she thought as she injected the creature. "I don't know if he was serious about eating him or not, but he had a pistol. And he shot at him. Luckily, I think the bullet only grazed his back leg."

"Oh, my gosh," she breathed, petting Nick's fur. "Does he need stitches, do you think?"

"No. Probably just a good bandage."

He closed his eyes and drifted off. "He's had a busy day. Who could have done something so terrible?"

"Do you know Ugo Telemaco?"

Concetta's jaw dropped. "Him? Really?"

"So you do know him?" Audrey asked, smoothing back the fur on Nick's leg so she could see what she was working with.

Concetta, seeing what she was doing, fetched the antiseptic and fresh bandages and medical tape. "Yep. My mother told me he used to run naked through the neighborhood, peeking in people's windows. And he would always walk around town with a little red wagon, full of junk, so that people thought he was homeless. He's more than a little. . ." She twirled a finger by her head. "I didn't know he still lived around here? I thought the town kicked him out."

"He lives in a shack near the orange grove," she said, shuddering. All of that sounded absolutely insane. G had said he was eccentric, but she'd had no idea how bad he was. If she'd known, she probably never would've gone there. Leave it to G to see the good in everyone.

But Ugo wasn't good. He'd tried to kill her pet. Which only led her to wonder . . .

"By the orange grove? Do you think he had something to do with that murder?"

Audrey shrugged. "That's why I was there, talking to him. I'm pretty sure he was the guy I saw in the grove. But he insisted that he was near the area, heard the gunshots, and ran off, thinking someone was after him, and he got lost."

Concetta frowned. "Likely story. Do you believe that?"

"I don't really know what to believe. Knowing what I know about him, now, I think he's a pretty solid suspect. I should probably tell the police about it. He has a gun, he was in the vicinity of the murder when it happened, and he has a history of unstable behavior. In fact, if the police *haven't* been to his place, I'm concerned why."

"Right. Unless they don't know he's there."

"Possible. I should tell them, after work," she said, finishing the bandage on Nick's leg and cutting the tape. "Should be good as new in a few days. You should go home. There are no more appointments today. And I know we have a busy day tomorrow."

"Oh." Concetta's face fell. "That's what I wanted to tell you. Cancellations have been coming in like crazy. You don't have *any* appointments tomorrow."

"None? That can't be right." Audrey placed Nick in a bed for observation and went out to the front, where she stared at the following day's schedule on the computer screen. So far, four appointments had been cancelled for the day, and two for the day after that.

"That's odd, isn't it?" Concetta asked, pert nose wrinkling.

"Not if word is getting around that *I'm* the killer," she said with a sigh.

"You? Come on. Just because you were nearby . . .?"

"The outsider is *always* the killer. Don't you know that? Bambino's owner has probably been going around, passing the fear on to everyone else."

"Yes. Poor Bambino."

Audrey nodded. "I know. I keep wondering if he's okay. Or if she found another vet. Maybe all the cancelled appointments are taking their animals into Palermo? That's the closest veterinarian, from what I hear."

"That's a hike."

"Yes, but it'd be even worse if they think they can go without, like a lot of them did before I moved in. Or they use folk medicine and prayer instead of actual medicine. If animals don't get the proper medical care, I shudder to think what could happen."

She'd been there before. The people of Mussomeli were reluctant to let an American take care of their pets. Then, once she'd been accused of murder, the distrust had run rampant. It'd almost caused her clinic to fold up even before it'd gotten off the ground. It took lots of work to build and maintain that trust, but it seemed like every time she made headway, something pushed her back.

"But they're just rumors," Concetta said.

"One thing I've noticed . . . People around here take rumors as fact. They don't even bother to look into them to see if they're true. They just steer clear."

Concetta nodded. "Like that mafia rumor. I can't imagine that man will ever fit in among us considering the things people have been saying about him. It's sad, really."

Audrey nodded. "It is. That man at the Tivoli estate is very nice. And I asked him if he was mafia."

Concetta stared. "You did? What did he say?"

"Of course, he said no. He said he was aware of the rumors and they were ridiculous." Audrey shrugged. "But I suppose that's what he would say, even if he was involved in the mob."

"True. Even with the one-dollar house thing and all the new faces moving in, people are wary," Concetta said, but suddenly, her eyes lit up. "Oh, wait! Speaking of strangers, I have a message for you." She went to the computer and tore off a sheet of paper from a pad. "From a Rafael."

Audrey's ears perked up. "Rafael?"

"Yes. He said he wanted to speak to you in person, and to stop by his place any time tonight." She wrinkled her nose. "You know him? Who is he?"

Tonight. For dinner? Her skin prickled at the thought.

"He's the so-called 'mafia boss' at the Tivoli estate," she said, thinking. "The rich, handsome man who asked me to lunch."

"Oh! He's a Piccolo? Rafael Piccolo?"

"Yes. I was just down there, earlier this morning. I wonder what on Earth he wants to talk to me about?"

"Guess there's one way to find out?" Concetta winked.

"Okay, considering how busy it is, I guess I can close up early. I do want to ask him a question, anyway. Something about what Ugo said made me wonder . . ."

Concetta leaned up against the counter. "Made you wonder what?"

"Well, Ugo said that when he was out there in the grove before I got there, he heard two gunshots. But Rafael never mentioned hearing gunshots at all. He said he didn't hear or see anything. And I have to wonder . . . why?"

"Oh. That *is* a question." Concetta shrugged. "And I still want to know who made that anonymous call."

Audrey smiled and grabbed her things. "Me, too. But I'm not going to get the answers here. I'm going to get so much exercise, going up and down those stairs," she said, grabbing her purse and giving Nick a head rub. "I will see you later!"

CHAPTER FIFTEEN

The sun was sinking behind the city as Audrey made her way into the orange grove, shadows growing long, each one looking like a person, watching her. Even though it was still as hot as Hades in the valley, she shivered. Knowing someone had been murdered here, and that the murderer was still on the loose, was worrying enough. But the fact that Piccolo, who seemed nice enough, might be lying to her, was even worse. Not to mention that the neighbor was gun-happy. It gave the bright, citrus-filled valley a sinister quality.

Well, at least this time, you were invited, she thought as the tiled roof of the villa came into view.

She stopped and straightened when there came a faint rustling behind her. Turning, she noticed the leaves of a low, scrubby bush, rustling in a way that was too violent for the meager breeze. She took a step back. *Please be a squirrel.*

It stopped for a moment, and she was just about to turn and head on her way when the leaves parted.

Crouching there, staring at her with a curious look, was Nick.

"Nick!" she whispered harshly. "What are you—did you escape the clinic? How did Concetta—"

She gave up as he leapt over to her, clearly fine. He started to pull on his bandage, eager to get it off.

"Way to shake it off, Bub," she said, crouching and reapplying the bandage as best she could. "But you should still wear this. You don't want the wound to get infected. Come on."

The moment she dropped Nick's foot, he gave up with the bandage and started to head off on his own, after a fallen piece of fruit.

Audrey patted her thigh and whispered sharply, "Nick. Don't run off. Stay close. We've already proven this place is *not* safe for you, not with Mr. Crazy next door, wanting to make you into his next meal."

Dutifully, he fell in line behind her, staying at her heels as she made her way down the stony path, toward the house.

Moments later, she arrived at the stone archway with the gate to the main courtyard. As she stood there, wondering if she should knock or let herself in, she saw three men, striding through the courtyard. They were wearing dark suits, despite the hot day. They stopped right in front of the fountain she and Rafael had eaten in front of, only yesterday.

She hesitated there, feeling terribly out of place, wondering if she should be there at all. It felt like she was witnessing a business meeting, and she was completely underdressed, not to mention, not there for business.

One of them men turned to say something to another, wagging his finger in a slightly threatening manner. He had longish, dark hair, feathered on the sides, and black sunglasses. When he moved aside, Audrey saw a smaller, bald man, who had a face that looked as if it'd been in one too many boxing matches. The other man was Rafael. He threw up his hands and shrugged. He didn't look upset, but he did look rather *concerned*.

She leaned in forward, trying to understand what they were saying, but besides their voices being too quiet, she was pretty sure they were speaking Italian.

Rafael said something about a *problemo Italiano.* He kept repeating those words, *problemo Italiano,* over and over again. As he spoke, Audrey stiffened when she heard a car door slam. Rafael said something that she translated to, *"Giuseppe is here. Let's go in."* She was proud to find her translation was correct; they did, indeed, go in, toward the front of the house.

Leaving her wondering what the heck was going on.

She crept forward toward the side of the house, evading a rather prickly line of bushes as she went. The first window she came to was closed, a shade pulled tightly over it. She quickly bypassed it when she saw that another window, at the front of the house, was open, its shutters banging lightly against the side of the house in the breeze.

Audrey nearly tripped over Nick, trying to get over there, to see what was going on. Now, she felt even more ridiculous, creeping in the bushes. But she simply couldn't fight the curiosity. Stooping under the window, she could hear the voices, closer now. She slowly lifted her head to look inside.

The room was full of white plaster and dark stained wood. The floor was a cold terracotta tile, and the only furniture in the place were uncomfortable looking benches that looked like numerous church pews. In fact, all the décor of the place looked as though it'd been reclaimed from an old Catholic church. There were crosses and statues and religious relics everywhere. The one main window across the way was a stained glass one, which cast multicolored prisms on the walls and floor. Right in front of her was a large, well-stocked bar.

But the room itself was empty.

Still, she heard the voices. She realized they were coming from the front of the house. *Audrey. You were invited. So why are you skulking around among their bushes?*

Simple. She was frightened. And what if he hadn't invited her back for dinner? What if he'd heard she was snooping around and had invited her back to kill her?

Come on, Audrey. Don't be paranoid. If he was going to invite you back here to murder you, he wouldn't have told Concetta to pass along the message.

Taking a few steps forward, she peeked her head around the corner, just in time to see two sleek black town cars parked in the circular drive out front. Audrey crouched behind a flowering bush and watched as an older gentleman—who could have very well passed for Marlon Brando—approached Rafael and gave him a kiss on each cheek. The rest of the men did the same, then Rafael put an arm around the older man and turned to lead him inside.

As he did, she noticed a bulge in his side, underneath his black blazer. Was that . . . a gun?

Before she could confirm it, his eyes swept right across the space where Audrey was hiding. She quickly threw herself back against the side of the house, heart beating madly. *He has the same name as a well-known mafia family. He's friends with a number of men in suits. They kiss each other on the cheek and whisper solemnly about business that looks very shady, indeed. If that doesn't tell you these guys are mafia, Audrey . . . what will?*

She looked down at Nick. This had trouble written all over it. And she'd almost lost her beloved pet, because of her stupid curiosity. So what if Rafael had asked her to stop by? She'd seen enough. She didn't want to have dinner with him, or have *anything* to do with him, whatsoever. She needed to stop this.

She began to bend down to scoop him into her arms when a voice, nearly at the back of her neck, boomed, " *Posso offrirti da bere o qualcosa?* "

90

It might as well have been a voice saying, "Stick 'em up!" because Audrey's hands flew up. She looked up to see nothing but the open window, and the very top of Rafael's head. Seconds later, she heard the sound of ice cubes, clinking into a glass, and some liquid being poured.

Then she translated. *Can I get you a drink or anything?*

She relaxed. *Oh. He's talking to his guests.*

At that moment, though, her throat was so dry, she wished she could have something to drink, too. She closed her eyes, pressing herself as hard as she could against the side of the house to make her body as small as possible. All she needed was for him to lean out the window and see her, crouching among the bushes.

He said something that she quickly translated. Something about agreeing there was a problem, asking what they were going to do about it.

One of the other men spoke. From the low, gravelly tone, Audrey sensed it was the older man. He even sounded like the Godfather. But Audrey couldn't make it out. Something about it being "unfortunate."

Then she heard Rafael's voice, farther away from the window, now. *"Andiamo a bere di fuori, nel cortile."* The resulting footsteps and voices, trailing away from her, made her realize that he'd asked them to go outside, to the courtyard.

The sane part of her tugged on her, telling her to run away, as far and as fast as she could. But another part of her, the part that eventually won out, begged to find out what unfortunate thing they were talking about. And what was this *Italian Problem?*

She crept back toward the gate to the courtyard, stopping at the stone wall and listening. As she did, she heard Rafael say, quite plainly, *"No. Non ho voluto io questa guerra."* No. *I did not want this . . .*

She frowned. *Guerra.* What was that word? She couldn't remember ever hearing it before.

One of the other men, the younger man with a squeakier, less self-assured voice, spoke. He said, *"Non capisci in che guaio finirei? Potrebbe mettersi molto male per noi."*

Male. Bad. She was pretty sure that he was saying, *This could be bad for us.*

But what was it? She had to get closer. Looking around. She found a protruding stone in the wall and used it to lift herself up so that she was peering over the wall, behind some tall evergreen bushes. Nick easily scaled the wall and sat next to her. She leaned closer, intent on

91

hearing their next words. The short, unfortunate-faced man growled, *"La guerra sta arrivando fin qui."*

There it was again, that word. *La Guerra.* Whatever it meant, it was coming. *Sta arrivando. It is coming.*

"Troppo vicino," the young one said. *Too close.* *"Quell'uomo era solo il primo."* *He was the first.*

The first what? And what man?

Audrey's skin prickled. Were they talking about the dead man? The victim?

No, they're not, Audrey. Don't get crazy. They're probably talking about another man.

Then Rafael said, *"Si. Lo so."* *Yes, I know.* *"E tutta questa situazione prenderà una brutta piega... in capo a un attimo."*

She squinted. That, she was totally lost with. *This situation will get . . . worse?*

Frowning, she lifted her backside so she could reach into her back pocket and retrieve her phone from her shorts. As she was pulling it out, someone said the word *Guerra* again. She navigated to her translating app and started to type it in when Rafael said, *"Uccidere Grinnelli è stato stupido."*

She looked up. *Uccidere.* She knew that word.

It meant "murder." *Killing Grinnelli was stupid.*

She stifled a gasp, her blood running cold.

So that meant one thing. Rafael had lied. He knew far more about the death of that victim than he'd told police. There was a familiarity there, as if he'd known the victim. In fact, it sounded very much like he knew exactly who'd killed him, and why.

Eyes widening, Audrey finished typing the word and pressed "return" to get her answer.

As she did, a voice in front of her said, *"Dottore Smart?"*

She looked up to see Rafael, curiously eyeing her from her perch atop the wall. He tilted his head, confused.

"What are you doing up there?"

For a moment, she thought of scurrying down, but as she moved to do so, she lost her grip on her phone and it tumbled down by her feet, into the bushes surrounding the courtyard. As she reached down to grab ahold of it, it bounced from her fingertips and disappeared into the bushes . . . and she followed, slipping into the prickly bushes, practically head-first.

One of the last things she saw before she fell was the translation of the word *Guerra,* on her display.

It meant "war." And she had a feeling she'd invited it to her doorstep.

CHAPTER SIXTEEN

The next thing Audrey knew, there were footsteps sweeping across the stone courtyard. Audrey looked up to see Nick sitting what looked like miles above her, staring down from the top of the stone wall. He had his head tilted, like, *Humans. What good are they?*

She tried to move, but the thorns of the bush had trapped her. She reached around for something to pull onto for leverage, but she was frozen in this spot, her legs slightly more elevated than her top half, in a thorny bed of brambles. Nothing hurt too bad, though. Except maybe her ego. Her cheeks were burning; she already knew she was going to regret this, big-time.

That is, if she survived.

Seconds later, a quartet of male faces appeared above her, Rafael among them. He reached for her, helping her to standing, and said, "*Dio,* what were you doing?"

Too humiliated to speak, she reached down and wiped a leaf from her shirt. They were all looking at her. She averted their eyes, wondering if she was in for it. Had it started with Pietro Grinnelli, the same way? He'd just innocently stumbled in on their dastardly plans?

But Rafael smiled warmly at her, in a way that instantly relaxed her. He said, "When I invite people over, I usually expect them to knock on the front door. Or at the very least, come through the gate."

He pointed at it. She tried to smile, but her teeth were chattering. "I'm sorry. I tried to. But the gate was—um, stuck. So I thought I'd just—" She pointed to the wall with a shrug, as if it was a totally reasonable alternative, and not completely ridiculous.

The young guy, raising a skeptical eyebrow, went to the gate and tried the latch. Of course, it opened easily. He murmured something in Italian under his breath that Audrey wasn't sure she wanted to understand.

"Oh. That's crazy! It totally didn't work for me!" she said with an innocent shrug. "I've never been that good with things like that."

Then they all looked at her accusingly, except Rafael, who was still smiling in amusement. He put a hand on her shoulder, but she instantly stiffened. *Is he usually this nice right before he pumps his victims full of lead?*

"Relax," he said to her amicably, then looked at the other suits. "Doctor Smart, here, is the town veterinarian. She lives in the center of Mussomeli. American. She and I became acquainted yesterday, right, *cara?*"

Audrey nodded.

"Well, are you alright? Nothing broken, I hope?"

She nodded, wiping stray strands of brown hair from her face.

"You certainly known how to make an entrance." He eyed the steep wall. "So you were really just trying to get in?"

"Yes. I know it was silly." She tittered. "I did call to you, but I guess you didn't hear? And I heard voices, so . . ."

He reached into the bush and pulled out her phone. He stared at the display for a moment before handing it over to her. Of course, the display had her translation of *Guerra,* right there, in black and white. If he had noticed it, he didn't let on. She wiped off the display and pocketed it. "So, um, yeah. I'm here because you invited me. My assistant said something about . . ."

Rafael snapped his fingers. "She said I invited you?"

Audrey nodded. "Yes, she—"

"I'm sorry. I did not."

Now, she felt even more foolish. "You didn't call the clinic?"

He shook his head. "Unfortunately, no. That's all right. Thank you for coming, *Dottore.*" He motioned her forward. "But please don't think you need to leave right away. Let's stop standing in the bushes. Why don't you come over and have a drink with us?"

"Well—"

Before she could say any more words of objection, he'd ushered her toward the fountain. Marta was there, now, doling out more drinks and appetizers for the guests. Audrey felt a little better, upon seeing the woman. *They wouldn't kill me in front of her, would they?*

She hoped not.

"So someone pretending to be me asked you to come out here?" He asked, stroking his chin. "Curious, eh?"

"Y-yes," she stammered, feeling even more foolish. Did she think she was lying? That she'd come here, just to spy on him? If so, she was done for. She could feel it. Her whole body was trembling. "Honest."

"Oh, my dear. You've had a day. Please. Sit. Catch your breath." He sat her in a chair and said, "Allow me to introduce my family."

"Oh, you are all family? Now I really should go." She tittered. "I didn't mean to disturb you if you were having a family reunion--"

"Nonsense. You are welcome here."

She looked around. Judging from the expressions on their faces, he was the only one who seemed to think so.

"This, here, is Giuseppe, my uncle." He threw an arm around the Godfather lookalike. "He's as near and dear to me as my father, God rest his soul." He looked up at the sky, and they all did the same, crossing themselves and kissing their fingers.

She waved just the tips of her fingers at Giuseppe, who bowed very politely. *"Incantato di incontrarti."*

Rafael leaned in a bit toward her. "Forgive him. He says he's enchanted. He does not speak any English."

Was he really Rafael's uncle? Audrey couldn't tell. They didn't really look anything alike. "Oh. Nice to meet you."

Rafael motioned to the two other men, the young, baby-face one and the older, bruised-faced man. "And those two ruffians are my . . . cousins. Franco and Rocco. They have just come in for the day, to visit me."

Audrey tried to smile as nonchalantly as possible, but when the older one—who she thought was Franco-- lifted a hand to wave, he bared what looked like the very end of shoulder holster, under his jacket.

Audrey didn't have much family, so she couldn't be sure, but since when during a family visit was it necessary for anyone to pack heat?

Her blood ran cold at the thought. "Uh . . . nice to meet you."

Frowning at her, they muttered half-hearted *Ciaos,* but Audrey couldn't shake the feeling that they wanted her gone. By whatever means necessary.

And if they were mafia, then she really couldn't put it past them to pull out their guns and shoot her dead, right there, with no pretense. Just like what had happened to Pietro.

She started to shiver at the thought and went to cross her arms in front of herself to keep from shaking visibly.

"Ah. You're scratched," Rafael said suddenly, grabbing her hand. She looked down and realized she had a small trickle of blood on the underside of her arm.

"Oh, it's no—"

"Marta!" he called, straightening. *"La cassetta di pronto soccorso, portamela!"*

A moment later, Marta scurried out with a small first aid kit. Rafael opened it and pulled out some antiseptic, then gently cleaned the cut with a cotton ball. *Well, maybe this is a good sign? He wouldn't patch me up if he was just going to kill me, right?*

Still, it felt odd, sitting there, as all the men stood around her in a semicircle, watching Rafael inspect the cut like a surgeon about to make the first cut.

"This really isn't that bad, just a—"

"Shh," he said as he stooped over her, fussing over her wound, acting as her nursemaid. With the blood cleared, it was barely a scratch. Hardly worth the attention he was giving it. She felt a little like a pampered princess as he inspected the wound more closely. He blew gently on her skin to dry the antiseptic, making her skin alight with goosebumps, then rummaged in the bag for a bandage. Carefully, he unwrapped the bandage and applied it, then patted her knee in a loving way. She blushed under his attention.

Meanwhile, the other men watched, their movements clipped and a bit annoyed. The tension was off the charts, as if the whole place was a powder keg, ready to blow at any second. She knew it was because she was there, and because they wanted to get back to whatever they'd been discussing before.

Also, because they didn't trust her.

And one of them had killed Pietro. After what she'd heard, she was sure of that.

Which meant they probably wouldn't bat an eyelash at killing her, too.

But right now, Rafael was *tending* to her, with just as much tender loving care as she used with her own patients.

When he finished, she gently pulled her arm away from his grasp, feeling awkward, but not wanting to upset him. "Thank you. Much better. But I'm sorry. I'd better be going. It's busy at the clinic. I am sorry to have bothered you."

She jumped up, as if propelled by a cannon.

"No bother, like I said. Are you sure I can't offer you a drink?" He raised an eyebrow.

"No. Really. Thanks," she said, backing away. She backed herself into a column, and nearly tripped over the low stone edging around the garden, and almost walked herself right into the same wall she'd fallen from, earlier. But no way was she going to turn her back on them.

She'd seen what happened to Pietro.

She managed to fumble with the gate and slipped through, still smiling, though her insides were rioting. They watched her the entire way, not speaking. The moment she was free of them, she broke into a run, Nick at her heels, climbed the staircase in record-time, and didn't stop until she was back at the clinic.

CHAPTER SEVENTEEN

Breathing hard, Audrey leaned over, trying to get the blood to rush to her head. Nick stood close by, looking at her in that same dubious way.

"Sorry. I'm not a runner. I'll never be a runner," she huffed out, still feeling like she was dying.

The door to the clinic was locked, now. Finally, Concetta had given up and gone home. Audrey fished for her keys in her purse, unlocked the door, and went straight inside to the water cooler in the break room, where she sucked down an entire glass of water.

She fanned her face, still feeling like she was dying. Of course, it was probably better than two bullets in the back.

And that was what she'd been dancing with. She felt sure of it. Sure, Rafael had been nice and congenial, but maybe he didn't call the shots. Maybe that old guy, Giuseppe, wanted her dead. Maybe they'd come after her, in the dead of night . . .

Calm yourself, Audrey reminded herself as she paced, still trying to catch her breath. *This isn't Goodfellas. You didn't do anything wrong. You're likely fine.*

Even so, when she went back into the darkened hall, she did so cautiously, half-expecting to see a man in a dark suit, standing at the end of it, gun drawn.

Of course, there was no one there. *Stop being silly and go check on the animals. Everything's fine.*

She went toward the kennel, but stopped in the hallway, close to the reception area. Then she rushed forward and twisted the lock on the door. Just in case.

Feeling better, she walked back to the kennel to check on the animals. The dogs yipped and the other animals stirred excitedly in their cages as she approached and turned on the light. Concetta must've gone through, cleaning their cages, prior to leaving, because there was very little to do.

She took a kitten out of its cage and gathered it in her arms, slowly stroking its fur. She did it more for herself than for the animal, since petting a warm-and-fluffy always seemed to calm her down. The kitten purred contently, making Audrey feel more relaxed.

Was Rafael really a murderer? Was his "family" mafia? She went over the many things she'd overheard, shuddering as she replayed them in her mind. They could've killed her. She had no idea how close she'd come to dying.

And who had called her, pretending to be Rafael, asking her to come down to the villa? That was very odd. Someone seemed to want to get her in trouble.

But who? And why? To take suspicion off of someone else?

Maybe Rafael *had* called her. Maybe he was denying it just because he knew that her snooping around the place would make her an excellent suspect.

Her mind whirred with the possibilities as she stood there, alone. She felt like she needed someone to talk to. But Concetta had gone above and beyond. And G? Mason?

No. Just no. Doing that would only give her more problems.

What I should do is call Detective Dinardo. Leave it in his hands and be done with it. That's what any normal person would do.

She set the kitten down in its cage, closed the door, and walked to the front reception area. She picked up the phone from its cradle and hesitated.

But what if Dinardo is working with them? And he tells Rafael you were the one who reported their suspicious activity? Then you will REALLY be done for.

She set the phone down, pulled her cell phone from her pocket, and called the only person she could think of. Luckily, she answered right away. "Aud, are you really calling me at an actual, normal time, and not in the middle of the night?"

"What time is it there?"

"Three PM. I just put Byron down for his nap."

"Aw. How is Byron? The twins?"

"Fine. They miss you. But I'm sure you didn't call at such a *normal* hour to ask me about them."

Audrey smiled at her sister and tried to keep her voice as even as possible. "Don't worry, Brina. I won't make it a habit. Tomorrow, I'll call you at three A.M."

Of course, her big sister saw right through her brave façade. "That's better. Is everything okay?"

"Well—"

"Let me guess. You're having to choose between *Signore Hotness* and Mr. Dreamy Abs, and you can't decide."

She gritted her teeth. If only that was the biggest problem on her mind. "Actually, no, it has nothing to do with Mason and G."

"Oh? Bleh. I really was looking forward to helping you weigh the pros and cons of them."

"We've already done that, about a thousand times," she muttered. "And it hasn't helped much. But I'm actually calling about a situation that's even more confusing."

"*More* confusing? All right. I'm intrigued. Lay it on me."

"All right, well. . . I was down in an orange grove yesterday, and I met a man named Rafael, who owned the villa there. And he was very nice. We had lunch together and—"

"Stop it. Stop it. Are you saying you don't have a love triangle? It's more like a love square?" She squealed. "I love it! You go! He even has a sexy name. *Rafael*. So he owns an orange grove? So that means he's rich. Is he as hot as the others?"

"No . . . no . . . no, wait. You don't get it."

"I do get it! I know men! And he asked you to lunch! Sounds like a love connection to me."

That was true, Brina did know men, very well. And yes, she had been asked to lunch. But after that was where the Greatest Love Story Ever Told went *completely* off the rails. "Hold on, Brina. Let me tell you everything before you go telling me where I need to go to get the wedding invitations."

"Fine. Go ahead." Audrey heard her sister breathing out forcefully through her nostrils. She was probably biting her tongue to keep from blurting more questions.

"Okay, so. On the way home from lunch, I was walking, and I found a dead body in the grove," she said, rather nonchalantly, probably *too* nonchalantly for what it was, but at this point, she'd had enough time to process it and, really, the dead man wasn't the point. The point was the fact that she was, once again, a suspect for a crime she didn't commit. That kind of thing was getting old, fast. She'd freaked out enough; she didn't have any more time for hysterics.

"Uh . . ." There was a pause. "What did you say?"

"A dead body."

"Again? Really, Aud? You keep wanting me to visit you there . . . why again? It sounds like a war zone. I'd probably end up a casualty. Isn't this like, the fifth dead body you've found?"

"I know, I know. Really, Mussomeli is very safe. But listen. It was lying in the grove. The man had been shot."

"Oh, my God . . ."

"Yes. And so the police came, and looked into it, and well . . . certain things have happened, and well . . . I think Rafael might be . . ." She leaned in and cupped her hand around the phone. Silly, really, because there was no one there. But what if they'd bugged her phones? Criminal types did that, didn't they? "Mafia."

"What?"

She realized that if they had bugged her phone, they'd be able to hear her, regardless of how loudly she spoke. She said, a little louder, "Mafia."

"You are not serious."

"I am."

"What makes you think so?"

"Well, I was sort of, hanging out around the grove today, and he was meeting with a bunch of suits he called 'family.' And I'm pretty sure they had guns. Plus, they were saying something about a war, and an Italian problem, and I don't know Italian really well, but I think they had something to do with the murder."

"Oh. My. God. *Oh my god oh my god oh my god.*" Another pause, within which Audrey wondered why she'd told Brina about this. Brina may have been a wizard when it came to men and the dating scene, but she wasn't exactly big on all things crime related. Now, she'd probably just worry. "What are you doing, on the phone with me? You need to call the police!"

"I know. I was going to, but then it hit me. You know these small-town cops. What if the mafia bought them? What if the police are in their back pocket? If I call to tell them what I witnessed, they might—"

"Oh, come on Audrey. That only happens in movies. They can't possibly have the police in on it with them," she said surely. "You need to call them. They don't think you did it, do they?"

"Well, I did find the three other bodies here, so—"

"Yeah, but you don't even have a gun! Do you even know how to *fire* a gun? You probably have never even *touched* one before."

"Right. But they don't know that. And they're always suspicious of me. So I guess you could say I'm reluctant."

"Well, I wouldn't hesitate to go there and tell them what you know. Right now. Go! Do it. And call me to let me know how things went. All right?"

She smiled. "Okay. I will."

"Audrey. Be careful. I love you."

"Love you too, sis," she said, ending the call. She set her phone down, trying to summon the courage to march herself down to city hall and the police station.

But it turned out, she didn't have to. When she looked up, she saw a body, hovering in the doorway. It was Detective Dinardo, and he didn't look happy at all.

*

When she looked up to see Dinardo, he was just raising his knuckles to rap on the door.

She jumped up and scurried around the reception desk to answer. When she opened it, she got the look from the grave expression on his face that whatever he was about to tell her was not good.

"Hello, Detective," she said as she opened the door wide, allowing him to pass through. As he did, Nick slipped in as well, then climbed onto one of the chairs in the reception area and made himself at home, licking his paws. That meant, *Dinnertime, human. Or did you forget?*

"Hello. Burning the midnight oil, aren't you?"

She shrugged. "Not really. I was just finishing some things up, but I was on my way home." She motioned to a chair next to Nick and sat down herself, across from him. "Can I help you with something?"

He nodded. "It's about the body you found."

She swallowed. She assumed that much. And now was the time for her to tell him everything she'd seen today, especially the little bit about Rafael and his "family". Instead of speaking, though, she swallowed again. She would tell him. *After* he told her what he had to say. "What about it?"

"Well, we've discovered more about the identity of the victim, Pietro Grinnelli," he said, reaching into his breast pocket of his blazer and pulling out his pad. "It appears that the man was from the mainland, Italy, and that he had ties to the mafia there."

"Mafia, really?" Audrey said in surprise, as her mind went back to the men in suits, quietly discussing. They'd said there was an "Italian Problem."

Was Pietro the Italian Problem?

And what did that mean? Had they had him killed? Threads of ideas fired through her mind, but she couldn't grasp a single one.

"Yes, do you happen to know anything about that?" he asked, watching her closely.

"No . . . why would I?" She frowned. "I'm an American. What would I know about the mafia?"

"You did have lunch with the man who owned the estate, did you not? This Rafael Piccolo?"

She nodded.

"Did you find anything out? Where he came from, what his business is, what he's doing here?"

From that line of questioning, it certainly didn't sound like Dinardo was in cahoots with the mafia. She shook her head. "Wouldn't you be better off asking him that?"

"Perhaps, but I thought . . ."

"We just chatted, mostly, about inconsequential things. He didn't tell me anything, really, about himself. He spent most of the time talking about his estate. I guess it's been in his family for years. So that's why I'm a little confused—Mussomeli is a small town where everyone knows each other. You didn't know the Piccolo clan?"

"Of course I knew them. Everyone knew them. They were run out of the town in the early eighties, when the police caught wind of some illegal business they were doing. Back then, yes, there was rumor that they were mafia. But then they disappeared, went underground, I don't know where. All the Piccolos left. And now they're back. All I have on them is this past history, and a dead body," he said, sighing. "Nothing else to tie him to the murder. But if what happened in the eighties is any indication, I get the feeling that it might be the first dead man, but it won't be the last."

Audrey shuddered. "What happened?"

"All kinds of shady things. My father was on the police force at the time. He was constantly going over there, because of something or another." He leaned forward. "I don't think it's a good idea that you've been over there so often. They are bad news, *Dottore* Smart. Very bad news."

104

"So . . . *often?*" She repeated the words as something dawned on her. She hadn't noticed anything or anyone else, because she'd come from the path behind the house. But was it possible that there were officers watching that she hadn't noticed? "Are you surveilling the house?"

He didn't answer but stared at her a beat too long so that she knew the answer was yes.

"So you think Rafael did it?" she asked. "He murdered that man? Why?"

He nodded. "He's in the old family business. And in my experience, people get murdered by the mob for one of two reasons— one, because they betrayed the family, or two, to *keep* them from betraying the family."

She shuddered. Probably climbing over a fence and spying on them was a bit of a betrayal. It was a miracle she wasn't sleeping with the fishes, now, but it all made sense. Pietro Grinnelli had seen too much. Maybe he was going to squawk to the police. But then . . . Rafael caught wind of it, thought their extensive network of informants, and . . . lights out.

She was about to say, *I think you may be right,* and tell the detective what she'd seen, but then he added, "And I think he had help."

She pressed her lips together. Yes, his "family" certainly seemed close. If he'd had help, it was likely from one of them. They seemed angry, and more than willing to help Rafael when needed. Family was important above all else. They looked out for each other. Did it matter which one? She supposed it did. As she sat there, frowning, trying to decide whether it was Rocco or the other one, whose name escaped her, who likely pulled the trigger, she caught sight of Detective Dinardo, staring meaningfully at her.

And then she understood. She patted her chest. "You think *I* helped him?"

He shrugged. "It's possible. You were right on scene. Didn't hear the gunshots. There are about a dozen holes that I could tear in your story. It just doesn't make sense."

She let out a gasp of exasperation. "What part? I told you, I don't have a gun. If he wanted help, he could've asked his family."

"Family?"

105

"Yeah. His cousins, Rocco and Blocko, or something. I can't remember. They're probably better at this than I am, being career criminals, and all."

He nodded. "But they didn't arrive here until this afternoon."

She stared at him. "Well, don't you know everything about them? It's a wonder you didn't already solve the case." She shook her head. "I know nothing. I did nothing. I promise."

"Did you ever think it was engineered that way? That Rafael did it and made you come to lunch with him, because he knew you'd at least say that you were together?"

"Is that aiding and abetting?"

He said, "No . . . because you've been there too many times, Dr. Smart. Which makes me think that you know far more than you're letting on. I think you two knew very well that this murder was about to happen, and you did nothing to stop it. In fact, you encouraged it."

"But what motive did I have?" she asked, once she'd picked her jaw up off the floor.

"It's simple. You two are both newcomers. Perhaps you were acquainted before. In a relationship? And you're covering for one another. Your stories don't add up."

This would be the part where she would tell him what she'd overheard, at the Tivoli Estate, earlier. But the detective was off his rocker. She couldn't believe what he was saying. "Covering for one another? Do you happen to remember how Rafael was practically accusing me?"

"Maybe. But then he has since changed his story to say that he thinks you were nowhere near the body when it was found."

"He has?" Well, that was nice. But he was just trying to backpedal because she'd yelled at him for placing suspicion on her, instead of telling the truth. If everyone would just *tell the darn truth,* this wouldn't be a problem. Now, she felt like she was stuck in a web, where the more she tried to free herself, to more hopelessly entangled she became.

"I do find it very unbelievable that you were out there and never heard the gunshots. I think you know exactly where the weapon is."

She shook her head. "I don't. And I promise you, I didn't know the man until I went to his estate yesterday."

"Right. When you received an anonymous call." He sounded doubtful, so there was no way she was going to tell him about the second anonymous call that brought her to the estate, earlier that day.

"It's true. It happened. And I know the Piccolo clan even less than you do. You're grasping at straws, Detective."

Instead of arguing her, which she was sure he would, he said, "Hmm. Yes. Well. It does appear that Rafael has an alibi. According to his housekeeper, she spoke to him right before she heard the gunshots, so there was no way he could've gotten that far. And even though he has the family background . . . his record is very clean. Squeaky clean."

That made her feel a little better. "See? I told you. If I were you, I'd stop wasting time looking at me and Rafael's family and look at that neighbor. Ugo. He's a menace, and if he hasn't already killed someone, he will, soon."

"Ugo . . ." He burst out laughing. "Ugo Telemaco? He's just a crazy old recluse."

"But he has a gun. And he was in the grove at the time. I saw him."

"Is that so?"

"Yes, he was wearing polka dots at the time. That was why I went down there, the second time. G told me that he wore strange clothes like that, so I decided to have a look myself. And when I went to check on it, he pulled out a gun on me!"

The detective seemed to be trying to keep a straight face, but then a small smile crept onto his lips. "I'd say that serves you right."

"It's not funny! He nearly killed Nick!"

He looked over at Nick, who looked sullen, upset that he hadn't had dinner yet. He stroked his jaw, then wrote something in the pad and snapped it closed. "All right. I'll be looking into this, interviewing more people. But if you do have anything you'd like to tell me about Rafael Piccolo, I'm all ears."

She'd wanted to. She'd wanted to tell him everything that she'd seen, and about the "Italian Problem." But now, she felt like anything she told him would only incriminate her, more. He seemed dead set on the fact that she was involved.

So she simply nodded and said, "Thank for coming by."

When he left, she looked at Nick, who mewled softly, wanting his apple. "I suppose the only way I'm going to prove myself innocent is if I can prove Rafael innocent as well," she said, scooping him into her arms. "But fat chance of ever doing that, considering there are all those mobsters around, not to mention, the police are watching."

The only problem was, what if Rafael Piccolo *wasn't* innocent?

Grabbing her things, she went outside, locked the door to her clinic, and headed toward *Piazza Tre,* hoping no mafia men lurked in the shadows, waiting for her. Even though her mind wasn't on it in the least, she had renovations to get to.

CHAPTER EIGHTEEN

"I hate you," Audrey breathed, shining her light up at the living room wall.

This wall was even worse than the first one, and she'd just spent the better part of the week filling all the divots in it so she could plaster it over and have a nice, smooth surface to paint. But the second wall looked like an archer had been using it for target practice. That wasn't an exaggeration.

In the background, Van Morrison crooned from her iPhone about sailing into the Mystic. She balled the ugly flowered wallpaper, tossed it in the trash heap, and wished she could sail away, leaving this all behind, while little gnomes fixed everything for her. That would be nice.

That's what lucky Nessa, across the street, had. She'd yet to see Nessa even break a fingernail.

But there's something to be said about doing it all on your own! she told herself, echoing something her father, the contractor, used to say. *It feels good to get your hands dirty.*

She looked at her hands. They were very, very dirty. And there was no end in sight.

Once I'm done with this wall, only two more to go, she thought bitterly, grabbing the tub of spackle and her tools.

She'd thought she was lucky, getting this massive house, one of the nicest dollar-homes in Mussomeli. She had an idea of how it was going to look—pale blue, with wainscotting and some dainty Baroque-period furniture she'd seen in an antique store on *Barcellona*. But the one thing she hadn't thought of was how much more work it would be to get to that point. The kitchen and rest of the lowest level had been easy, because they were small. But this room was so big, like a ballroom. It felt like this living room was never going to be done.

Mason said he'd help me.

She took a sip from her glass of wine, then slopped a little on the first divot in the very bottom corner and sighed, preparing for a long, long night. *No, no, no. Don't even think of it.*

As she smoothed it on, getting into a little groove, she felt better. All things were better with a little wine and some Van Morrison.

Suddenly, she heard a loud bang outside, then screaming.

Nessa.

She jumped to her knees and went to the large picture window, then pushed open the shutters to find the camera crews. Nessa was wearing a robe, her wet hair up in a towel turban, and screaming at two very remorseful-looking men quickly packed up their gear. "I told you seven A.M!" she growled. "Not P.M!"

One of the men, a bald, overweight man in jeans and a polo who Audrey was sure she'd seen before, grabbed his camera and threw it in the open back doors of the van.

"Let me have that!" She screamed, reaching for it. She grabbed the camera and yanked it toward her, all the while punching numbers into her phone, one-handed. "I'm calling my agent. The last thing I need is videos of me, indisposed, showing up online. If they do, I'm going to come for your head!"

The man started to explain himself, but she cut him off with a death glare.

"I don't care! I wasn't expecting you! I—" She cut off as someone must've answered the phone, because she said, "Lon. Get control of these barbarian camera crews! I didn't know they were coming, and I think they filmed me when I wasn't expecting it!"

Welcome to my world, Audrey thought, closing the shutters before Nessa could catch sight of her and focus her laser eyes on her.

Then she turned around and smiled. Nick was there, excitedly playing with an apple core, trying to get the last bits of flesh from it. The room would be lovely and light when she finished. And best of all, she didn't have any camera crews following her every move.

She started to smile, until she remembered the police, following her every move. If they were doing it to Rafael, Dinardo would probably be following her, soon, too. After all, they were supposedly, "in it together."

But eventually, they'd find out she had nothing to do with it, right?

She wasn't sure. But she sure didn't want to go back to the Tivoli estate, with all those mobsters.

Which reminded her. She hadn't asked him the question about whether he'd heard the gunshots.

Not that it mattered. It was clear he'd lied about a lot of things. He'd probably only lie to her about that, too. What she needed to do was stay clear of Rafael Piccolo, let the police do their job, and eventually allow them to clear her name.

Well, I have plenty of work cut out for me, here, she thought, gazing up at the massive, ancient wood-and-iron chandelier above her. It was more cobwebs than anything else and would need to come down and be refinished. Later.

"Knock knock," a voice called from outside. "Boston? You there?"

Mason.

Her heart did a little flip in her chest.

She called, "Yeah. Come in. I'm up here. In the living room."

The door swung open and Polpetto appeared, rushing as fast as his gangly body could muster on the slippery tile. He bounded up the stairs to Audrey and licked her face. "Okay, boy. Hi, there. I missed you, too." She cupped his giant face in her hands and gave him a kiss. As she did, Nick started to hiss. "Oh, stop it. I don't have time for this."

By then, Mason was climbing the three short steps into the living room. He looked around, hands casually in the pockets of his jeans, nodding his approval. "Getting there."

She snorted. "Right. At this rate, it'll be done by the time I'm in dentures."

"Told you I'd help."

"You've helped me too much. I feel terrible. Free vet exams for Polpetto for life doesn't even begin to compare," she said, draining her glass. "Wine?"

He shrugged. "Sure."

She went down to the kitchen, where she found a slice of pie, waiting for her. "What's that?"

"Pecan pie. Had a hankering for it."

"Thanks, that's mighty kind of you," she replied in her best Southern drawl. She got another glass down and poured them each some wine.

He took his. "What do we toast to?"

She sighed. "I don't know. I can't think. It's been one of those days."

"That bad? So . . . let me guess. They haven't figured out who killed that guy, and so they're still up your butt?"

"Bingo. You're good. How did you know?"

He shrugged. "This actually isn't the first murder you've been accused of, remember?" He took a gulp of wine and swallowed. "Not to mention, I saw a police car going down the street while I was walking here. They were going really slow, looking up at your place."

"Really?" She went to the window and looked out. It was dark except for a single streetlight, across the Piazza. No police officers. No mafia men, either. All was quiet. "Well, they're gone now."

Mason sat down at the bistro table in her kitchen. "So what's the deal? And why do they still think you did it, instead of that possible mafia guy that owns the grove? I think he's a *little* bit of a safer bet." He raised his thumb and forefinger up, apart an inch. "Did you find out anything else about him?"

She nodded. "It's so weird. I thought he'd summoned me there, so I went to talk to him. And then it turns out he hadn't. But while I was there, I heard him talking to a bunch of men in suits, and it was really creepy. I could've sworn I heard the theme from The Godfather, playing in the back, as they talked. They were speaking in Italian but I'm pretty sure they said something about a problem that they got rid of. The dead guy."

He raised an eyebrow. "I sure as heck hope you got out of there, as soon as you could."

She winced. "Well, I kind of . . . fell into their garden."

He winced in response. "And they noticed?"

She nodded. "But then he was really nice. He brought me over, patched me up. Offered me something to drink. He was very hospitable."

Now, a new expression appeared on Mason's face. It was part disgust, part concern, and a little bit of pride mixed in there. "He was, was he? And you took him up on it?"

"Well, only long enough to be friendly. Then I got out of there, as quickly as I could."

"Smart." He leaned back in his chair. "Just because he doesn't look like Marlon Brando doesn't mean he's all rainbows and sunshine, girl. You've got to—"

There was a sudden knock on the door. She exchanged a look with Mason, hoping it wasn't G. *Like I need my life to be any more complicated right now.*

She went over and pulled the door open. No, it wasn't G.

It was worse.

It was Rafael.

CHAPTER NINETEEN

Rafael Piccolo was standing there, in his dress shirt and slacks, sleeves rolled up to the elbows, smiling at her. "*Buona sera,* Dr. Smart," he said in a low voice.

"Mr. Piccolo!" she said in shock, sensing Mason stiffening behind her. "What are you . . . I didn't realize you knew where I lived."

He shrugged. "I asked around. Are you very busy? I am sorry to bother you so late."

"Oh, well—"

Mason stood up and tweaked her shoulder. "Who's this?"

"Uh, this is a . . . friend," she said. "Rafael, Mason. Mason, Rafael. Mason was just leaving."

Mason crossed his arms. "No, actually, I was—"

She glared at him and mouthed, "*Leave,*" her eyeballs shifting toward the door.

"But—"

"*Please*? I'll call you later."

He studied her for a long time before relenting.

"Apparently, I was just leaving," he muttered. "See you later, Boston."

Mason stood several inches taller than Rafael, a fact made obvious when he brushed past Rafael in the doorway, eyeing him with unblinking suspicion.

Ridiculous, but maybe that was what he thought. He got similarly defensive and started acting oddly when G was around, too. But there was absolutely no reason to be. Hadn't she just got done telling Mason she was pretty sure he was mafia? Like she'd ever be interested in *that*.

But then another thought came to her mind. Maybe he was just trying to protect her from the mafia guy.

Oh, that made more sense.

It was too late, though, because a second later, she was alone, with Rafael at her front door, watching Mason walk away from her.

Was he upset at her? He wouldn't admit it, but probably. "Wait—Mason . . ." she started.

He didn't turn around. She fought the urge to run after him. That would probably only make things worse. Besides, she was exhausted. She couldn't deal with *one* man, much less two.

Rafael smiled after Mason. "Friend of yours?"

She nodded, remembering what she'd promised herself—that she wouldn't go associating with any potential mob bosses. Otherwise, it'd only make the police more suspicious. She peered out at the dark street, but only saw Mason, rounding the corner and heading out of sight. "You surprised me. Is there something I can help you with?"

He reached down and lifted a large basket that she hadn't noticed, until now. It was filled with oranges. "I felt terrible about you hurting yourself today, so I came by to offer you this and see how you are?"

"Oh, that's very nice." She took the basket and looked over her shoulder at her meager place. It was nothing like the gorgeous mansion Rafael was used to. *I should invite him in, now, but do I really want to be alone with him?* "I appreciate it."

"You're welcome."

They stood there, awkwardly, for a moment. He didn't make any movement that suggested he was going to retreat. Clearly, he *wanted* to be invited in.

"Um, well—I'd invite you in, but renovations have my place in a shambles righ—"

"That's fine, *cara*. I've seen worse." He took a step forward so that she had no choice but to step aside, letting him through. When he stepped into the kitchen, he looked around. "Ah, a citrus lover. Lemons! I love it!"

She smiled, then quickly scuttled toward the bistro table to take the empty wine glasses from her previous visitor. The basket of oranges was so large that it dwarfed the small, two-person tile-topped table. She motioned for him to sit, and he did so, sliding into a chair with grace, crossing his one leg atop the other so that the ankle rested on his knee, making himself at home. He was wearing loafers with no socks, a look that Audrey had never liked. She averted her eyes from it and grabbed the bottle of wine. "Can I get you—"

"No. No, I can't really stay."

Could've fooled me, she thought. It was a good thing he declined, because the bottle was nearly empty. She set it in the sink and turned to him. "Was there something else I could help you with?"

115

He shifted in his seat. She half-expected him to reach into a pocket and pull out a small pistol. But instead, he said, "I must apologize for how rude my family was to you."

Oh, was that it? "Not a problem. I'm from Boston. I'm used to much ruder people than that. Trust me."

He chuckled. "Ah. They can be intimidating to most people. I'm glad to hear you weren't intimidated."

She wouldn't go that far. She clearly remembered being so intimidated when the quartet of them had stared over her in the garden that she'd nearly wet herself. But it was all water under the bridge. She hoped. She'd survived. So far.

"All is good," she said with a smile.

More awkward silence. It seemed as though he was fishing for something, but she didn't know what, until he said, "That was some fall you took. I hope you are all right?"

She nodded.

"What . . . again . . . what were you doing up there?"

Oh, so that was what he was after. "I told you. I thought I'd been invited. I was just trying to find a way in."

He nodded slowly, as if it made perfect sense. Which, of course, it didn't. It was a patent lie, but it seemed like Rafael Piccolo was absolutely fine, dancing around the truth. He'd lied to her before. He looked down at the ground, pensively, and said, "That's right. That's right."

Audrey snorted. She'd never liked lying, and from the beginning of this conversation, something inside her had begun to bubble, like a volcano, getting ready to blow its top off. Finally, she exploded. "No, it's not right."

His eyes snapped to hers. "What do you mean?"

"You know what I mean. And you know why I was there. I was listening. And my Italian may not be all that great, but I heard what you were saying."

Both eyebrows shot up, wrinkling his forehead. "What was I saying?"

"You were talking about an Italian Problem. And a war. And that man from the mafia. You knew him," she said, her voice surprisingly calm. "You know him, because you and your family are part of the mafia. You lied to me. Admit it."

Her heart stopped as he stared at her, unblinking. She thought for sure that this would be the moment where he pulled out his gun and sent her to sleep with the fishes. But instead, he chuckled. "Well, you come right out and say it, don't you?"

"It's true, isn't it?" she pressed.

He let out a sigh of exasperation. "Yes. I suppose it is true. Though no one is usually that direct about it with me."

She blinked. So there it was. Her suspicions confirmed. Suddenly, she really wished she hadn't asked Mason to leave. Was this one of those, *I'd tell you, but then I'd have to kill you,* things? "I did ask you before, quite directly, and you said you weren't. But you were lying."

Laughing, he said, "That's why I like you. You're the only one. You don't like to play games. You go after what you want."

She rolled her eyes, unimpressed by the flattery. "Is it true? Are you mafia?"

He shrugged and then nodded. "Guilty as charged."

She expected relief to accompany the revelation, but now she felt even more dread. She'd been falling for a mafia man. A killer. And now she'd basically cornered him and forced him to admit it. In the mafia's book, that probably meant she was one thing: A liability. Someone they needed to get rid of, and quickly.

But she couldn't stop now. She'd pulled the lid off, and now was the time to grab onto what was inside.

"You killed him, didn't you? You killed Pietro Grinnelli."

He shook his head and said, quite definitively, "No."

"You didn't? But you told the police that you'd been walking in the grove all morning, and you never mentioned hearing gunshots or anything."

He nodded, stone-faced. "All right. I might not have been in the *grove all morning.* In fact, I heard the gunshots and ran out to see what the problem was. And that was when I ran into you. At first, I thought you were one of them, but you seemed too flustered to be. So I thought lunch would help calm you. " He smiled placidly.

Audrey's mind whirled, and doubt seeped from her voice as she said, "I don't understand. You really didn't do it? And you have no idea who did?"

"I don't know. I saw no one else, but you."

"One of your family?"

117

"No. They only arrived today, after I called them, to help me deal with what's going on."

Her lips twisted. "Then who?"

He shrugged. "That's what we're trying to figure out. We know the Grinnelli clan. They've been our enemies on the mainland for over a century. But we've been out of each other's hair for most of the past two decades. We don't know why he came out here, what he wanted."

"You don't? You mean, he never stopped by the house, or anything?"

He shook his head. "Marta said no."

"So you mean he'd come all the way over from Italy to randomly wander through your orange groves? That sounds really suspicious."

"I agree. And we all agree that it's put the town in an unfortunate situation."

"Yeah, I'll say. We've already had a few other murders in recent months. We don't need more," Audrey said, thinking of how Brina had reacted when she'd heard about another murder in Mussomeli. "It's not good for bringing in more dollar-house-buyers."

"Not just that." He pressed his lips together. "The Grinnelli family is very powerful. And no doubt, they've already heard of the murder. So I can promise you, they're probably getting ready to take the next ferry over and get some retribution."

Audrey's jaw dropped. "That's not good."

He nodded. "I wish I knew who did this foul thing. Because if the Grinnellis think the Piccolos did it, a war will be coming."

A war. *Guerra.* So that was what they were talking about.

"And you are sure it wasn't any of your men?"

He nodded.

"You're not lying?"

"No. No, I know that it wasn't a Piccolo. And the reason I know is because we left Palermo because we wanted to step away from that history. To leave our evil heritage behind. That is why I'm here, and why many of my family members scattered around Sicily. We want peace."

"Did you tell the Grinnellis that?"

He shrugged and a smile touched his lips. "Yes. But they're a little like you. They're so used to us lying that they'd never believe a true word we said."

A shiver went down her back. She wondered briefly if Falco and the town council knew anything about this. "This isn't good. If the Grinnellis come here and wage war on the town . . ."

"I know. I know." He turned his hands to the ceiling, then stood up. "It means I probably shouldn't be speaking with you. And we shouldn't be in town at all. I don't want you or anyone else in this town to get caught in the crossfire."

She crossed her arms, now a little more relaxed that he wasn't going to pull out a gun and try to end her life. "So, why did you come, then? Just to find out what I know?"

"Actually, I did it because I think about you, often," he said, his eyes glimmering.

Her mouth dropped open again. Handsome men, dropping by to lavish gifts on her and check up on her. Why had she never had this problem in Boston? "Oh . . . really?" she asked, still doubtful.

"And I was wondering what you thought of me. But now I know. You think I'm nothing but a lying crook. And you're right."

She opened her mouth to argue, but then she thought better of it. He was right, after all. Her response was far less impassioned than she'd planned. "I don't think you're *that* bad."

He stood up, went to the door and opened it, a sad smile on his face. "Nevertheless, I'll stay away from you. For your safety. Enjoy the oranges. Consider them a parting gift."

"Thank you. Good night," she said, closing the door behind him.

She turned back to look at Nick, now not interested in continuing on with her renovations at all. The wine was going to her head, and now she had so much more to think on. Rafael was mafia. She'd gotten herself involved with the mob. And Rafael seemed to want to keep her safe, but was it too little, too late? And how could she believe anything he said?

*

When Rafael left, she stood there, in the dying light of the sun, thinking about many things, but mostly about the choices that led her to this point. And yes, she felt a little sorry for herself. *I'm so stupid. How do I get myself caught up in these things?*

She definitely didn't have an appetite for doing more renovations. Not now. Not to mention that her head felt fuzzy from all the wine.

Her stomach growled, rousing her from her thoughts.

Dinner. Dinner would be good.

Turning back to the house, she realized she had no food to speak of. That is, except for Mason's pie and a load of oranges. While she ordinarily wouldn't have minded dessert for dinner, her stomach craved something savory, not sweet.

She wanted some of the specialty of *il Mercado del Pepe—Macco di fave,* their delicious bean soup that always perked her right up. She'd practically lived on that stuff, and G's *ciambotta,* ever since her plane touched down in Sicily.

She looked at Nick. "Come on. I'll get you an apple. My treat."

She pulled the door closed behind her and peered up and down the empty street. From her stoop on *Piazza Tre*, she could just look over and see the orange trees in the distance, melting into the dull pink light of the setting sun. Something seemed to pull her toward it, but she resisted, starting on her way toward Pepe. *Don't bother, Audrey. Someone else will find the murderer. You need to stay out of it.*

She walked along the crooked street, yawning as she dodged in and out of shadows cast down from the streetlights. As she turned onto *Barcellona*, she waved at a couple of locals that she recognized. Instead of waving back at her, they moved to the other side of the street as she approached.

She groaned. *This is crazy. It seems like the whole town already thinks I'm married to the mob.*

As she approached Pepe Market, she noticed Luigi outside, pulling in the outdoor bins with that day's vegetables. *Luigi is a friend. He gives me free veggies all the time. At least he won't ignore me.*

She crossed the street, waving at him. "*Ciao,* Luigi! *Come va?*"

He didn't respond like he usually did, with a full paper bag of that day's treats. Didn't even look at her.

Her heart sank. Really, was she that much of a pariah that even people she considered her friends would ignore her?

It was only when she neared him that she realized he was staring, quite pale-faced and wide-eyed, into the window of his shop. He was gripping a tomato so tightly in his fist that it had burst, bleeding fleshy seeds on the front of his apron.

"Is everything all right, Luigi?" Audrey asked, peering through the window.

"No," he snapped, his voice full of anger.

That was when she caught sight of the two men from the orange grove, through the glass. Rocco and Whoever, Rafael's cousins. They were at the cash register. The shovel-faced one had a pastry crammed between his lips and was fishing in the pockets of his blazer for money. Carmen was checking them out, looking at them with an expression identical to her husband's.

"Oh," she said. "You know those men?"

He didn't look at her. He continued to stare through the window, as if he expected he'd have to go in and save his wife from them. "I don't know them, but I know their kind. They wear their suits and expensive wristwatches and stick out like sore thumbs." He spit on the ground. "They're a bad kind. They don't belong here."

Audrey watched as the two men finished paying and, both sharing a private joke and grinning from ear to ear, stepped outside. When their gazes fell upon Audrey, they looked at her with suspicion, which turned back into amusement as Luigi shouted something at them in Italian. Audrey didn't know what, exactly, but she got the feeling it wasn't exactly PG-rated, because the hand gestures definitely weren't.

The young one fired something back, his eyes dancing. Luigi threw down his bucket of tomatoes and started to lunge, but Audrey put a hand on his shoulder, holding him back. "Easy, Luigi. Remember what you told me about not getting tangled with them?"

He looked back at her and nodded. "They're no good," he repeated, shaking his head. "Cosa Nostra."

"Right. They do everything in the middle of the night. No witnesses. So watch yourself."

But it's still daylight, at least, for a little while, she thought, as the two men headed up the street, toward the clinic, looking like they owned the town as they fished fresh powdered-sugar zeppoles from a paper bag and noshed on them. Audrey watched them, wondering just what their part was in this. Had they really arrived after Pietro's death, or was Rafael covering for them? Or maybe they'd murdered Pietro, and Rafael didn't know?

The questions burned inside her, making her shift uncomfortably. *They're not as old or as bright as Rafael. If I could just ask the right questions, maybe they'd give something away . . .*

"*Si,*" he said as she helped him pick up the bucket of tomatoes. "You should stay away, too. I heard word that you've been messed up with them. Tell me it is not true."

She sighed. "It's not," she said, but that sounded like a lie. "It's not *technically* true. I got called out there by an anonymous tip and found the body, so I'm kind of in it. I've been trying to stay out of it, but it seems like the more I try, the more tangled I get."

"Si. That's mafia for you. Once you're in. You don't get out." He shook off his grave expression and said, "Can I help you with anything? More soup?"

She nodded, staring the way the men had walked. "Uh—yes." She smiled. "Actually, you read my mind!"

"Coming right up," he said, walking to the door. He noticed Nick sitting there, begging like a dog with his little paws up, and handed him a shiny red apple. Nick's tongue wagged with excitement as he bit into it.

She hesitated there, still looking up the street. "You know, I think I might have forgotten to lock up the clinic. You mind if I just go there and meet you back here in a minute?"

"Not at all. I'll have it all ready for you when you return."

"Thank you. And thanks for the apple," she said, heading up the street, toward the clinic. She distinctly remembered locking the clinic a few hours before, but she couldn't shake her curiosity. What where the cousins doing?

But as she walked, she looked around, unable to see them anywhere. The two cousins had disappeared, it seemed. She checked her watch. In another half-hour, it'd be dark.

At her clinic, she stood at the stoop and admired the way her name looked, painted on the window. *Dottore Audrey Smart, Veterinaria.* She never got tired of seeing that.

As she stared, a streetlight above blinked on, and she caught sight of something in the reflecting in the glass of the door.

The two cousins were sitting on the edge of the fountain across the street, facing her. *Watching* her.

The blood inside her ran cold. She sucked in a breath and reached for her purse, her first instinct to go inside, draw the shades tight, and hide under the reception desk.

Then she shook off the chills as a little girl skip-roped past her with her mother. *Don't be silly. This is not some mafia movie. And even if it is, they do their evil in the dead of night, with no witnesses. Right now, it's daylight, and there are dozens of people around. You're safe.*

122

She stood there, though, pretending to look in the window but still watching them in reflection. One of them leaned over and said something to the other, and they both laughed.

Audrey hesitated there for a moment. *Well, why not? You have questions. They have answers. And it's daylight. Nothing bad happens in daylight.*

Spinning she stalked toward them, into the street. She was so intent on the two men and the questions she was about to ask that she was nearly crippled by a Fiat, heading down the narrow street. It slammed on its brakes and the driver honked the horn.

"Oh, *Scuzi*," she said, tapping the front hood lightly as she navigated around it. She checked for Nick, but he'd already crossed safely, so she resumed her march. The men were still laughing, but now she knew it was at *her.*

The older of the cousins—the one whose name she couldn't remember—said something in Italian, in a rather cheeky, sing-song voice. She knew he was making fun of her, so she didn't bother to translate.

She crossed her arms in front of her. "What are you two doing in town? Does Rafael know?"

The older man snorted and gave her a thorough eye-raking but stayed silent.

The young one—she was pretty sure that was Rocco—laughed, grabbed a coin from his pocket, and tossed it into the fountain. Then he said in very broken English, "He is not our mommy."

The older man motioned with his chin to Nick, who was busy nibbling on his apple. "Is that yours . . . that rat?"

She inhaled sharply. "It's not a rat. It's a fox," she said, wondering why she felt the need to explain the obvious to a man who was just trying to give her a hard time. "Rafael would not be happy. He said that he didn't think any of you should be in town. You're going to cause trouble."

The older man laughed harder. "And what do you know about it?"

She leaned in forward and whispered, "I know that if the Grinnellis are in town and they see you, they're going to come after you, and innocent people in this town might be hurt or killed."

That made the man's smirk disappear in a flash. Rocco nearly choked on the powdered sugar of his zeppole. "Did Rafael tell you that?"

Whoops, she thought. Maybe that little tidbit was supposed to be just between them. She shrugged. "I know that the Piccolos and the Grinnellis are enemies. Everyone knows that. One of their men was found, murdered on your property. I think it's only logical that they'd be coming for retribution, wreaking havoc on this small town."

The older man scowled. "We had nothing to do with that murder."

"You think the Grinnellis would believe that?" she fired back. "Everyone on the island seems to know the beef your families had with each other. I'm surprised the police haven't already arrested him. And you two, hanging out here, making a scene--"

"We're eating a snack."

"Yes, but you look different. Face it, you don't fit in here. People are talking. Rafael came here to live, to—" She paused, almost saying what he nearly had, which was *lie low.* "To blend in with the residents, become a part of the town. You two are sticking out, and it's going to cast suspicion on him. Not to mention that just about everyone is talking about the Tivoli Estate, so the second the Grinnellis arrive in town, the residents will point them right over to it. Is that what you wanted?"

Rocco leaned in and whispered something to the older of the cousins. He shrugged. Reluctantly, they stood up to leave. Before they did, the older man came up close to her, too close for comfort. He stared at her for a long time before saying, "Again. We had nothing to do with that murder."

The way he said it, she almost believed him. But how could she? He was mafia. They lied for a living.

"Wait," she said as they began to walk away. They turned. "If you didn't do it, then who do you think did?"

They both shrugged. Rocco leaned in and said, "No idea. We arrived *after* murder. Rafael, he call us." He put a finger and a thumb to the side of his face, like a phone receiver.

"You really did?" She gnawed on her lip. Either they were really good liars, or they were telling the truth. "And do you believe Rafael when he says he didn't do it?"

The older man laughed bitterly. "Our cousin is a man of great honor. Of course."

"Then who do you think could've done it?" she asked them, now completely confused.

He came up closer to her, his hand patting the weapon under his blazer, and said, "The Grinnellis, like the Piccolo family, has many enemies. Take your pick. All we know is it was not us. But if war comes to us, what choice do we have but to defend ourselves?"

He turned and walked away, leaving Audrey shivering. She wasn't so sure she believed Rafael, but she really didn't believe these men, either. These men were trained in crime. They lied easily, as easily as they breathed. They could have murdered Grinnelli to start this war, and she could very well be playing right into it, like a fool, without even knowing. *I'm in over my head,* she thought.

And as she walked back to her home, checking over her shoulder every few minutes, she had the feeling she was only going deeper.

CHAPTER TWENTY

They do things at night, under the cover of darkness. No witnesses.

That thought was in Audrey's head as she made it to her front stoop, quickly unlocked the door to her house, and went in with her *Maccu di fave*. Nick scampered in behind her and seemed to sigh with relief, just as she did, when he was inside. She turned on a light and threw her back against the door, heart beating like a drum. After being out in the dark, with the mafia running amok on the streets of Mussomeli, her home felt even more like a sanctuary.

She yawned as she spooned the soup into a bowl. Then she sat at the bistro table with a glass of water—she was sick of wine, by now—and downed the soup. All the while, she glared at the oranges.

I don't even like oranges, she thought, wondering what she would do with a hundred of them.

When she finished her meal, she yawned again. So much had happened that day, she couldn't believe it. She climbed the stairs to bed, Nick at her heels, got changed into her pajamas, brushed her teeth, and crawled into bed, expecting to be asleep in seconds.

Of course, that didn't happen.

She watched the moonlight, scraping across the plaster wall opposite her, and thought about Rafael. How long had he been active in the mafia? Had he killed people? What other terrible things had his family done? And . . . had he really just shown up on her front stoop with a bunch of oranges, hoping to get to know her better?

Yeah, Brina would've just loved it if she brought him home to the States with her. She nearly laughed at the thought. *You had Signore Hotness and Mr. Dreamy Abs, and you chose the Mafia Don. You really know how to pick the winners, Aud.*

Wait. Was he a Don? Or . . . was he something else?

Scooting out of her bed, she grabbed her phone and Googled "Sicilian Mafia". It brought up a long Wikipedia page, entirely devoted to the island's rich mafia history. There was a thick section of the Piccolo family, too. Though Rafael's name wasn't mentioned explicitly, the Piccolos had once had factions in towns all over the island, and were noted for money laundering, racketeering—all the typical crimes that most regular, law-abiding people couldn't define. Of course, there had been murders, too, even a large-scale assassination in Palermo in the 1960s. The Don, Salvador Piccolo, was extremely powerful, and had dozens and dozens of important people in the police, the government, and public service, on the take. But he'd been murdered in the 1990s, by none other than the Grinnelli family.

There was a photo of him—a heavyset man with a pronounced moustache and familiar eyes. Salvador Piccolo looked very much like Rafael. Was he Rafael's grandfather?

It was so fascinating, she nearly got lost, researching it. There were pages and pages of crimes, associations, events, dates, murders . . . it went on almost forever. When she finally poked her head up from the rabbit hole, she realized it was almost midnight. Nick was curled up by her side, snoring loudly. She nudged him a bit to get him on a quieter cycle.

She wished she only had the problems with G and Mason, or the renovation, to figure out. Now, she had mafia stress on her hands. Why couldn't she just walk in the other direction? Why did she keep having to get herself in the thick of things?

She set her phone down, pulled the covers up to her chin, and rolled over, hoping she could sleep.

This time, she was just beginning to doze off when she heard a small noise, a bit of a cracking sound, downstairs, in the kitchen. Ordinarily, she'd have thought it was the house settling, but when it came again, louder, Nick's ears perked up and he stood at attention. Then he raced for the stairs.

She groaned. "Nick. Get back here. It's probably just a—whatever."

When he didn't return, she sighed and threw off the sheet covering her.

"Fine. I guess I'll go see what it is," she muttered, climbing out of bed. As she did, rubbing her eyes, she could've sworn that Nick let out a bit of a menacing growl.

Oh, great. Another mouse.

The moonlight streaming into her bedroom did little to light the narrow stairwell, so she navigated down each narrow step slowly, gripping the wall for support, since she had yet to install a railing. When she reached the second-to-last step, she fumbled at the wall for the light switch, peering through almost pitch-blackness. The only thing she could see was two shining pinpoints—Nick's eyes. He was sitting on the kitchen chair, still as could be.

"What's wrong, Bub? You lose the mouse?" she asked, finally locating the light switch. She flipped it on. "That isn't like y—"

She froze when she realized that Nick wasn't sitting on the chair. No, there was a human there.

"Oh sh—" she started, finishing with, "Sugar. What the . . .?" as she grasped at her madly beating heart and pressed herself back against the wall.

In contrast, the intruder was placidly stroking Nick's fur, as if he hadn't just broken into a private residence. She had locked the door before bed, hadn't she? The man, frowning, was large, older, wearing a dark suit, and . . . familiar.

It was Giuseppe. Rafael's "uncle."

He hadn't liked her yesterday, and judging from the disgust in his eyes, he seemed to like her even less, now.

"What are you doing here?" she whispered hoarsely. "You nearly scared the buttons out of me!"

His frown deepened, and he stopped petting Nick and shooed him from his lap. As she did, she noticed the bulge at his side, under his blazer. This was not good. She'd seen this in a movie, once. If it wasn't a horse head in the bed, it was a late-night, unexpected visit. *They do things at night, under the cover of darkness. No witnesses.*

He said, "*Veterinaria.*"

"Yes," she said, remembering that Rafael had said he didn't speak any English. Her eyes darted toward the side, to the front door. Could she get there in time before he drew his weapon? "*Sì.*"

"*Audrey Smart.*"

She nodded and took one single step toward the door, testing it. He visibly stiffened. At that, she decided to take no more. "*Sì, che vuoi?*" *What do you want?*

You already know. He wants to kill you. You know too much.

As if to confirm the fact, he brought his hand to his sidearm and rested it there. Maybe Rocco and Blocko had told him of the little dust-up they'd had on the street, earlier. She braced herself.

Then he said, "You know why I'm here."

She blinked. "Oh. You can speak English? Rafael said—"

"I taught *him* English, when he was a boy," he said disdainfully. "He make a little joke."

128

"Oh." She let out a nervous giggle, even though the joke wasn't funny then, or now. "And you are here because . . ."

"Because you need to watch yourself. I saw you yesterday. I know your type. You are a *chiacchierona*. You talk." He moved his hand like a jabbering mouth. "Too much. And that is bad for us."

She swallowed. "Is that a threat?"

He let out a short laugh. "Not from me. I'm the last person you have to worry about, *bella.*"

She started to relax. "So . . . you're not here to kill me?"

"No. Of course not. But there are others in our business who do not like the people who chitter chatter all day long. And you will be wise to avoid them. Avoid all of us. You understand?"

She nodded. "The thing is, I've been trying to. But it seems like I keep getting caught up in it."

"You need to get yourself un-caught. Stop asking questions and keep your distance, *mi senti?* You can get hurt if you do not. This is not a war you want to be part of."

She'd been crossing her arms and realized now that she had goosebumps all over them. This was weird. Standing in her kitchen, after midnight, talking about her safety with the mafia capo who'd just broken in. She'd spent all her life thinking the mafia were evil guys, and yet the ones she'd met so far had been some of the nicest men she'd come across. He'd come all this way to warn her.

She almost told him that she wished he'd have picked a better time, one less prone to giving her a heart attack, but then she remembered her conversation with the cousins. They *needed* to lie low. "Thank you for your concern. I will try."

He stood up. "Good." He took a step toward the door, but hesitated. "I can only imagine what you must think about us. But Rafael is a good, good boy. I can promise you that Rafael and my boys had nothing to do with the murder."

"Then who did?" She asked, exasperated. By this time, she didn't expect an answer. So many people--Rafael, Rocco, Blocko—had sworn up and down that the Piccolo family had nothing to do with the murder. But when she asked this question, they all simply shrugged.

So she was surprised when he said, "Pietro Grinnelli may have been a Grinnelli, but he was a little like Rafael. Rafael learned from me. We were trying to keep peace. Pietro, he was not the worst of the Grinnellis. He wanted peace, too. According to my nephew, he said he had some information for Rafael, and had come here to deliver it. He never made it."

"Information? What information?"

He shook his head. "I suppose we will never know. But all I know is that it's not for you to care about. It's our business, and we will handle it."

"You're going to handle it when the Grinnellis come for payback, and there's a full-out mafia war on the outskirts of Mussomeli?" she asked.

He nodded. "I hope it will not come to that. But yes. We do not want to hurt innocent people."

He went to the door, opened it, and nodded at her before passing through. A second later, he was gone, disappearing into the blackness like a vapor, as if he'd never been there before.

She closed the door, and this time, made absolutely sure it was locked. By the time she climbed into bed, she was wide awake.

Was there going to be a mafia war, right outside her bedroom window? If so, she couldn't just let it happen. She had to speak to Rafael and end this, somehow, once and for all.

CHAPTER TWENTY ONE

Audrey yawned as she stepped outside to start the day, and blinked her bleary eyes in the sunlight, then downed a few strong gulps of the coffee she'd made to wake her up. She planned to go and talk to Rafael, after her one early check-up appointment that she needed to make it to. That is, unless there was a message on the voicemail, cancelling it, just like all the others had been.

"All right, Bub," she said to Nick, who was sniffing the ground curiously. "Keep me awake. Know any good jokes?"

He barely noticed her, so busy was he, sniffing whatever trail he'd caught. She would've rolled her eyes, but she didn't have the energy.

She'd barely slept, the night before. It wasn't just the upcoming mob war that was on her mind, though she'd made a mental note to say something to councilman Falco about it. It was so much more, all of it grating at her. The two men she couldn't seem to choose between. Poor Bambino, who she hadn't been able to help. As wonderful as life in Mussomeli had turned out to be, all of these recent problems made her wonder if she'd made a mistake, dropping everything in Boston to come here.

You question whether moving here was the right choice almost once a week, she reminded herself. *Get over it. Things will get better.*

And they usually did.

Once the murderer was found.

Which only made her more eager to find out who'd killed Pietro Grinnelli. Yes, she'd made a promise to stay away from the mafia, but sometimes, the only way over was through. Maybe she needed to perform a little sacrifice in order to get action.

Besides, if she could prevent a mob war in Mussomeli, wouldn't it be worth it?

The only problem was, how could she find the killer if she completely avoided the Piccolo clan, like she'd promised Rafael and Giuseppe? She had to butt out. That was clear. A mafia warning was serious business.

But the mafia hadn't taken into account that the police thought she was responsible, too. And so that meant she was already implicated.

Rafael and the rest of the Piccolos couldn't come into Mussomeli. She couldn't go into the orange groves. Maybe . . . just maybe she could find out the information about the murder without leaving the town proper. Maybe she could find everything right here, under her nose.

Suddenly, an idea came to her, an idea even better than begging Rafael to keep her out of the brewing mafia war. She rushed up the street toward the clinic, so fast that even Nick had a hard time keeping up. She found Luigi at *il Mercado de Pepe,* bringing out that morning's fresh fruits and vegetables. "Luigi!" she called, breathless as she rushed to him. "Just the man I wanted to see!"

He frowned at her. "You no listen to me," he said, pouting a bit. "I told you those men were no good, and the next thing I know, I see you talking to them?"

She winced. She hadn't realized he could see that far down the street. "Well, they were outside my clinic and I had a question to ask them. That's all."

He eyed her dubiously. "What do you need help with?"

"Yes!" She pointed to the bin of oranges outside his shop. It only made sense that someone was collecting them for sale, and that whoever was might have seen something at the grove that day. "I was wondering if you could tell me where you got them from?"

His doubt increased. *"Dottore Smart . . ."* he began in a warning tone.

She shrugged innocently. "It's not about the mafia! I just have a . . . keen interest in oranges." She smiled, knowing how foolish it sounded.

He waved her off. "I get all the produce from Bucci's wholesaler. On *via Milano.*"

"Milano?" Mason lived on that street. That wasn't far away. She checked her phone. She could probably get there and ask some questions before the clinic opened up. She rushed off, calling behind her, "Thank you!"

"You be careful!" he called after her as she rushed up the street, toward the clinic. *Milano* was only two blocks over. If she got there quickly enough, she'd have no problem making it back by nine. But as she reached the front door, she saw Concetta there, juggling her bag and her keys.

"Hi, Concetta!" she said in a breathless rush. "I think all the morning appointments were cancelled, but the nine. You mind if I run an errand afterwards?"

Concetta blinked, a little startled at first, but then smiled and tossed her hair. "Sure. You can leave now. The nine was cancelled."

"Oh, it was?"

She nodded. "I checked the voicemail from home. I hope you're not getting yourself into trouble, are you?"

"No . . . not at all. Just thinking about oranges," she muttered absently, crossing the street and heading past the main piazza, with the fountain. She reached the via, trying not to notice as people seemed to swerve around her, and then walked up the street until she found the wholesaler, a nondescript brick building with many bays for trucks, and burly men unloading crates of goods.

She slipped inside one of the open garage doors. There was a man there, with a flat cap and a moustache, standing by a small truck, full of orange crates, as it was unloaded. She walked up to him. "*Ciao,*" she said. "Did you just pick up those oranges?"

He studied her, chewing on a toothpick, an amused expression on his face. "*Americana?*"

"Oh, *scusi.*" She pointed to the oranges. *"Dove . . . avete . . . preso le noci di . . ."* Ugh. What is the word for orange?

He seemed to enjoy watching her struggle. Finally, he put her out of her misery. "*Arancia.*"

"Right. *Arancia? Dove . . .*"

He laughed. "Don't bother. I got the oranges from the grove outside. That's where I always get them. I've done it as long as I've worked here, some thirty years."

She blinked. "You did? You mean, from the Tivoli estate?"

"Yes, *signorina.*"

"But I thought the place was abandoned for a while?"

"It wasn't abandoned. It was just that no one was living there. They had someone take care of the grove, though. Brought in good money, I'll suspect."

"I see. Who?"

"Who what?"

"Who was taking care of the grove?"

133

He shrugged. "I never saw him. I think it was a company. I never dealt with them. The pickers they hired would fill the crates and load them up on the side of the road for me, every other day. That's all."

Audrey scratched the side of her head. If that was the case, there'd been pickers there. Maybe not when she'd been there, but in the morning of the murder. "So you have no idea what the name of the company was?"

He pointed to a crate at the back of his truck. It said, *DeLuca.* "That's the most I know."

"So you've been going there for thirty years. Have you noticed any strange things going on there?"

"Strange things? Yeah, plenty. Especially lately. It was a large property with no fencing and a boarded-up home. A lot of people went there that weren't supposed to be there, and I'm sure plenty of things went on there that weren't technically legal." He narrowed his eyes at her. "Oh, you've heard the rumors, haven't you? You're asking about mafia stuff?"

She nodded.

"None of that. When the Piccolos lived there, they were always pretty quiet and kept to themselves. That body they found out there was the first one that I know of."

"So you saw people on the property who weren't supposed to be there?" she asked.

"All the time." He pulled the toothpick out of his mouth and spit off to the side. "The pickers were the only ones who should've been there. They were mostly kids, I think. Twelve, thirteen years old. But then there were others . . .you know, thieves, transients. There was a poacher I kept seeing, again and again."

"A poacher?"

He nodded. "I assume he was a poacher. Don't think killing animals on private property is legal. But there was nobody there to stop him, so he kept doing it. Went by the name of Ricardo. Had a truck like mine, but with a red front."

"He was killing animals?" Audrey asked, horrified.

"Yes. Rabbits, mostly. Other small game. Sells them in the market at *Abruzzo.*"

Though the idea of hunting animals disgusted her personally, she understood that people had to eat. Understanding that necessary evil was what had kept her from becoming a vegetarian, all these years. But

134

little bunnies, with twitchy noses and fluffy tails? Her heart clenched at the thought.

Right about the same time, something occurred to her. "If he was poaching, then he had a gun. Right?"

The man only shrugged, but the answer seemed obvious. And if he had a gun, maybe he'd seen something and taken a shot, accidentally hitting Pietro Grinnelli. It was possible—probably more than possible, considering that when she was there, the shadows of the trees, swaying in the breeze, had made visibility in the grove difficult, even in broad daylight.

It was too good a lead not to check out.

"Where did you say I could find this Ricardo person? At a market?"

He nodded. "If you wanted to track him down, he's probably there right now. They're open only in the morning at *Abruzzo*."

"*Abruzzo*?"

"You never been there? It's on the other side of town. Probably not for a girl like you, though. It can get very rough there. Bad sorts of people."

Audrey blinked, surprised. And here, she thought the bad element of town was out at the Tivoli estate. She didn't even realize Mussomeli *had* a rough section of town. But it couldn't have been much worse than her place in South Boston. The people in her neighborhood, in the only apartment in the city she could afford, had been slightly questionable, too. "Where is that?"

The men who had been unloading his truck gave him the thumbs up, and he thanked them, then reached for the door to his truck. As he did, he pointed over her head. "Just keep going west and you'll run into it. But I wouldn't go alone. That's dangerous."

"I'll be fine. Thanks," she said, breaking into a run. *First, though, I need to tell Concetta where I'm going.*

She was out of breath by the time she reached the clinic, even though it was only a couple blocks from the wholesaler. When she rushed inside, the waiting room was depressingly empty, and Concetta was in the back, grooming a Pomeranian mix. "I see it's been really busy," she remarked. "I haven't missed anything?"

Concetta sighed. "Really. Paint drying is more exciting. The phones have been dead."

For the first time, she was happy about that. "Do you mind if I take a half hour to run another errand? I have to go the market on *Abruzzo*."

Concetta's eyes widened. "Why do you want to go *there*?"

"Why, is it bad?"

She shivered in disgust. "Yeah. It's gross. It's been around for centuries, so it's definitely . . . well, my mother calls it 'quaint.' But I think it's creepy beyond words! And the people there are a little *off*. Mostly, it's people selling old junk, like one giant yard sale. One of my aunts used to sell potions there. She thought she was a witch. You'll definitely find things there you wouldn't find anywhere else." She eyed Audrey carefully. "What are *you* looking for?"

"I'm looking for a man."

Concetta shook her head. "You already have enough men. And the only ones you'll find at *Abruzzo* are toothless and not right in the head."

"I have to go," Audrey said, lifting her bag onto her shoulder. "I think one of the men there might have seen something about the murder at the Tivoli estate."

She raised an eyebrow. "Really?"

"Yes. Well, I hope. So I really need to go and check it out."

"Yes, of course! Don't worry about anything here. I've got it under control," she said, giving the dog in front of her an extra treat. "But be careful!"

"I will." She headed out, thinking, *That's the second time someone warned me to be careful in the Abruzzo market. But it can't be that bad . . . can it?*

CHAPTER TWENTY TWO

Audrey kept walking, and walking, and walking, straight down *via Barcellona*. For some reason, she'd never realized how big this small town was. Luckily, it was mostly downhill, but she knew the walk back would be no fun. It was nearly eighty degrees, and almost noon.

I should get a bottle of water to make sure I'm well-hydrated on the walk back. Don't want to be dying in the street.

She knew she was getting close by the sounds and the smells. The roads were packed with traffic, so horns were honking, and people were yelling at one another. There was a strange odor wafting through the streets, possibly food, possibly garbage. Whatever it was, it was thick and foul, not enticing like the smells emanating from G's café. There were many people on the stoops outside, and yes, many of them were young men who didn't seem to have anything better to do. A couple of them catcalled Audrey as she walked by.

She ignored it, walking faster. The homes here didn't appear to be a part of the one-dollar deal, because it didn't look like any of them were under renovation. They were all crumbling, and some were merely wrecked, burned-out shells, reminiscent of a war zone. The whole of Mussomeli had looked old before all the new buyers had come in to renovate, but it hadn't seemed *this* bad.

Following the sound of an upbeat folk tune played on a flute, she reached the street that she assumed was the beginning of the *Abruzzo*, judging from all the tables set up, marketing various wares. It was, just as Concetta had said, a mish-mosh of many items, most of them old and obviously unwanted. Audrey walked past a table with nothing but creepy old dolls, many the stuff of nightmares. There was also a man selling all kinds of exotic spices—she smelled it before she saw it. Another old lady was sitting behind a table, selling nothing but old, rather shapeless and moth-eaten hats. She winked at Audrey as she went by.

Audrey shuddered. *Forget the bottle of water. I need to get out of here as soon as possible.*

She walked past a woman selling all kinds of colored liquid in jars. She was dressed a bit like a gypsy, in a loose-flowing caftan and skirt, with a headscarf. She beckoned to Audrey and held up the jar. *"Un incantesimo d'amore."*

A love spell? She already had enough men. Audrey swerved away. "No, I'm not interested."

The woman grinned, revealing a golden tooth. "Ah, but I think you are. This one doesn't attract lovers."

Audrey stopped and stared at the pink liquid, confused. A love spell that didn't attract lovers? "What does it do, then?"

"I sense you are in great turmoil. You don't know what you want out of life?" she asked, raising an eyebrow.

Audrey fought the urge to roll her eyes. She'd had her palm read many a time before, and she knew the drill. Fortune tellers usually said generic things like that, that could relate to anyone. Really, who *did* know what they wanted in life?

But then the woman added, "You have a choice in your life to make. Between two men who couldn't be any more different. Yes?"

Audrey's attention snapped to the woman. She stared at her, and then at the vial. "Did you . . . how did you know that?"

"I am Signora Carina. I know all."

Now, Audrey really did roll her eyes. "All right, but how did you—"

"If you want to know, this potion will give you clarity."

Right. While I grow an extra limb on top of it, she thought, but she couldn't seem to pull herself away. Maybe that was what she needed? "What's in it?"

"My special combination of herbs and spices, and of course, the magic." Her eyes gleamed. "Just don't let your little pets have it. It's toxic. It is the *Lupino*."

"*Lupino?*"

She nodded. "It is a powerful flower. You will see."

Audrey hesitated. She didn't really want to put in her body anything that was toxic to animals, but there were plenty of things that were fine for humans, but toxic to furry friends.

The woman said, "I wouldn't wait. I don't come here often. Once a month, at the most. I only come when I feel like someone is going to be led to me. Someone in need."

"Fine," Audrey said, rummaging in her purse. She could decide whether to take it and give herself a stomachache from hell later. "How much?"

"Twenty euro."

She handed the bills over to the woman, took the vial, and slipped it into her purse, all the while wondering what had gotten into her. She'd never been the type to be enticed by something that was so obviously a gimmick. She'd liked to have thought she was immune to the hard sell. But apparently not, she realized, as she walked up the street. She was actually already planning to drink the potion, tonight, before dinner.

Then someone knocked into her on the busy walkway, waking her back up in reality. She looked around and realized she was still in the market. This wasn't a place to let her guard down. Clutching her purse tighter, she realized the foul smell was thicker, now, and followed it to a stand where plentiful smoke was rising from an outdoor grill. There were furry animal pelts of all colors hanging from racks above. She noticed the truck parked behind the stand— with a red hood, just as the driver of the other truck had said. At the same time, she caught sight of what was on the grill.

Little rabbit bodies.

Her lips twisted in disgust as she went over to the stand, her eyes watering from the smoke as she tried to find the owner.

"Come posso aiutarla in questa splendida mattinata?" a jovial but gravelly voice said, coming out of the curtain of smoke. *How can I help you this beautiful morning?*

The man was a bear of a man, big and just as hairy. He was grinning helpfully, but she couldn't help but think the man was only being kind to make a sale. From his camouflage shirt and pants, he looked *just* like the type who killed small animals for fun.

But there was something else. Something she realized, just as she opened her mouth to speak.

No, he hadn't spoken in English, but she was sure of it.

It was the same voice as the anonymous caller who'd phone the clinic to inform her about the injured animal. "Ricardo?"

He seemed delighted that she knew his name. *"Si?"*

She stumbled over her words, but just a little less than she had before: *"Dove hai preso . . . questi . . ."* She pointed to the rabbits. *Where did you get these?*

The appeasing smile disappeared. *"Chi sei tu?"* *Who are you?*

139

She fisted her hands on her hips. If he was the anonymous caller, then she didn't have to speak Italian. He'd spoken English perfectly well. "Did you get these rabbits at the Tivoli Estate orange grove? Is that where you do your hunting?"

His eyes went wide. *"Tivoli estate? Eh?"*

She pointed in the general direction. "Tivoli. The large mansion outside of town with the acres and acres of orange trees. Were you there, hunting, two days ago?"

He hissed out a breath. Then he said, "So what if I was?"

"I don't know . . . just that it's not legal. And someone was murdered there that day, too. Did you know that?"

His eyes narrowed, and for a moment Audrey thought she'd gone too far, and he was prone to lunging over the counter, at her throat. But just then, someone called to him from the other side of the stand. Glaring at her, he turned, waved, and when he began speaking to the customer, his cheerful voice returned.

She watched him as he chatted with the customer, then silently ran her eyes over the rest of the booth. As she did, leaning so far over that she almost tumbled into the booth, she noticed it. A hunting rifle.

Was that the gun that was used to shoot Pietro? If she could just get ahold of it, the police could test it to see if the bullets matched.

You can't steal it, Audrey. It's huge. If you take it out of here, he's going to notice.

She tapped her fingers on the side of the booth, thinking about how she could remove the rifle without being seen. But then she saw something even better on the inside counter.

His phone.

Keeping an eye on him, she slowly and carefully reached in through the animal pelts and lifted it up. Luckily, it was unlocked. She quickly scrolled to the phone log and found exactly what she'd suspected.

Aha! She thought, pumping her fists in triumph.

He'd made a phone call two mornings ago to her clinic.

He was the anonymous caller.

The man filled a paper tub with some vile-looking brown stew, attached the cover, and handed it to the woman. That gave Audrey enough time to slide the man's phone back where she'd found it. As he continued to chat with the customer and collect her money, she quickly typed in and sent a text.

A moment later, he was standing over her. "I suggest you leave."

140

She planted her feet. "It all makes so much sense, now, though. You were out hunting, the day of the murder. You thought you saw an animal, since there's never anyone in the grove, so you didn't think anything about firing a couple of shots. And it went down. But then you realized what you had done. You shot a person. And maybe he was still alive, but you saw what you'd done and panicked. You made a run for it, calling me later about an 'injured animal' because you felt guilty and wanted someone to find him."

He was shaking his head. "No . . ."

"I saw your phone. You made the call."

"What call?" He stared at his phone, pocketing it. "What were you doing, looking at my—"

"The call. To *me*. I'm Audrey Smart, the veterinarian."

His mouth moved, but nothing came out. "It's not true-"

"You're going to deny it? The evidence is right on your phone!"

"Yes. I mean, no . . ." He sighed, flustered. Then he looked up at the sky and shook his head. "Yes. I made the call. I found the body. But I swear I did not kill anyone. I was out there, hunting. I didn't realize until later that anyone had moved in. I was hunting, minding my own business, when I stumbled across that man, lying there, face-down. And yes, I panicked. I ran off. I didn't know what to do."

Audrey rolled her eyes. She had a hard time feeling sorry for a murderer of small animals. How was that even a fair fight? "Then why didn't you call the police?"

He snorted and threw up his hands. "You know why. I was there, hunting on private lands without a license. I didn't want the police to know that. But when I got back to town, it hit me what I needed to do. That is why I called the veterinarian . . . er, I guess, that's you. I pass by that place every day on the way to the market, and I thought you'd be able to help."

"Right. Help the *injured animal*. But it was a *human* you shot and killed. And you just left him there to die. Only a very cruel person would treat life that way."

She felt vindicated, biting off every word with satisfaction, as if she was, in some small way, getting back at him for the poor animals he'd killed. The market was such a chaotic assortment of sounds and sights, overloading the senses, that no one even stopped to watch her accuse the man. Even so, he looked around nervously, and his voice was so low that she could barely hear him over the roar of the crowd. "I didn't murder anyone."

She smiled smugly. Ordinarily, she hated being the person responsible for sending anyone to jail, but something about this man, Ricardo, just rubbed her the wrong way. It might have been the helpless bunny carcasses, lying all over the place. "Right. It may have been an accident. But you still killed him, and then you left the scene of the crime."

"I may have left, but I *didn't*—"

"You can tell that to the police."

His eyes went wild. "Don't you dare—"

Before he could choke the threat out, she looked over his shoulder and spotted Dinardo, walking through the crowd, his eyes intent on her. She heaved a sigh of relief. "Too late. I texted them while you were helping that customer. And here they are."

He froze, then looked over one shoulder, then the other, in a panic. She waved to Dinardo, who started to jog over, grimacing slightly. *He's probably going to yell at me for getting involved again,* she thought. *But at least I know I have the right man.*

As Dinardo approached, she opened her mouth to tell him the whole story.

But before she could get a single word out, the man lunged over the counter at her, knocking the wind out of her as she stumbled back, stunned. Then, as she tried to catch her breath, he broke into a run. Dinardo reached for his gun, but the poacher was soon swallowed up by the crowd.

"Stop him!" she shouted, scrambling to her feet.

CHAPTER TWENTY THREE

Audrey jumped to her feet in time to see the back of Ricardo's bald head as he tore down the street, away from the market. She and Dinardo took off after him, dodging bodies. When they reached the edge of the street, they stopped, scanning the area for any sign of him. But he was gone.

"Split up," Audrey gasped. "You go that way, I'll go—"

"No. Don't be a hero. You stay here. This is not your business," he said back, turning down a street and heading down an alley. As he did, he brought his phone to his ear, probably calling for back-up.

She stared after him for only a beat. *Right. I'm just going to stay here and do nothing? I don't think so.*

Just then, she saw a flash of a bald head, slipping past her, back into the crowd. "Stop!" she shouted, taking off after him. He looked back at her for a split second before picking up the pace and slipping into the crowd.

She chased after him, weaving around people in the crowd and tightly packed stands and tables of junk and unique wares. Just when she got close enough to him, a bicycle whistled past her, making her stop in her tracks as he surged forward.

"Stop him!" she shouted, too frantic to even think of the Italian word for *Stop*. She kept running, all the while running out of breath. He dipped between two buildings in a narrow aisle, and she followed, getting closer.

When she broke free of the alley, she plowed straight into a food cart, nearly knocking it over. The owner of it started to scream at her, shouting over her half-hearted apologies. Keeping her eyes trained on him, she moved around the cart, the front of her shirt now spattered with some red sauce.

Now, he was far away, and getting farther. She could barely see him. She was losing ground, and her endurance was flagging. A stitch knotted in her side, and she clutched at it, feeling hope draining away.

Suddenly, it came to her. "*Fermare!*" she shouted breathlessly, but by then, it didn't matter. The man was too far ahead of her.

When she rounded a corner, she lost sight of him entirely. She spun around, looking for him. Looking for Dinardo. But all the saw were the faces of people she didn't know.

I've lost him! She sighed.

Suddenly, a voice screamed above the din. It sounded like a frightened child. *"Ratto! Ratto!"*

Rat? At that point, people scrambled away as if someone had announced "Fire" in a crowded theater, leaving an open path for Audrey to walk through. She found the big, bear of a man, scrambling, flailing his arms and legs to shake off the animal that had securely attached itself to his pant leg.

Nick.

"It's a fox, idiot," she said, nearing him and the gnawing animal.

"I don't care! Get it off! Get it off!"

As if a fox was any stranger than any of the other odd sights in this market? And the man shot bunnies. He shouldn't have been so disgusted by the sight of the fox, but this one was chewing on his leg like it was a drumstick. *Serves you right,* Audrey thought, hesitating before pulling him back.

The moment she did, Dinardo rounded a corner and stopped short. "Ricardo? What's this all about?"

His eyes shifted to Audrey, just as the fox let go and scuttled into her arms. She said, "He was in the orange grove, poaching animals, at the time of the murder. That's where he kills the rabbits he sells at his stand."

Dinardo's eyes narrowed. "Is this true?"

Ricardo nodded sheepishly. He was out of breath, too, doubled over. A small crowd of onlookers had begun to gather around, now, so there was no chance of escape.

"And he saw Pietro and thought it was an animal, but it was Pietro. He killed him. It was an accident, but—"

"I did not! I've been hunting all my life! I wouldn't do anything so stupid."

Audrey scowled at him. "But you're the one who called me. I saw his phone," she said to Dinardo. "Just check it. You'll see."

"All right, all right," he said pulling out his cuffs. "But you were still hunting illegally, and that *was* pretty stupid. So I've got to bring you in. And we'll get this other stuff sorted out later."

He snapped the handcuffs on the man, who didn't resist. Audrey looked down at her pet. "Good job, Bub. I'd say that you deserve an extra apple for that one."

Backup police cars arrived. Before Dinardo led the culprit away, he leaned into her. "How did you figure it out?"

She shrugged. "Just . . . asking around."

He snorted and nudged Ricardo away, toward the police car.

Audrey sighed, relieved. It was over. Finally. The killer had been found. Now, she was no longer a suspect, so she could go on with her life, and . . . probably apologize to Rafael for ever doubting him in the first place.

It would've been nice if Dinardo felt the same way about *her*. But whatever.

Officer Ricci popped his head out and began to converse with Dinardo. The two of them looked over at her, before Officer Ricci broke away from his superior and headed toward her.

The young officer grinned at her. "How did I know you'd be in on this?"

She smiled. "I guess I always seem to be in the wrong place at the wrong time. Let me guess. You need to take a statement from me?"

"You are getting good at this!" he exclaimed, looking at a woman wheeling a cart of what looked like rags. He grimaced, just as she was jostled from behind by another market goer. "You want to go downtown to headquarters instead?"

She shook her head. "It's fine. It shouldn't take very long," she said. "Hey. How is Bambino? Did your mother get help for him?"

His face fell. "No. Poor pup still sick. She took him to vet in Palermo but—" He shook his head. "He's no better. If anything, he's worse. And in such pain. I tell her she should put him out of his misery, but she attached, you know?"

"Oh!" Audrey clutched at her heart. The one small consolation she'd gotten from Mrs. Ricci taking Bambino to Palermo for his care was that maybe they would find out what was wrong before she could, and that he'd be doing well by now. They had more up-to-date technology and better facilities, after all. She'd almost taken for granted that the little dog was better. Tears sprang to her eyes. "I'm so sorry."

"*Si*. Me too. My mama . . . she's beside herself."

"Well . . . maybe if you tell her that I had nothing to do with the mafia, she might let me take another look at him?"

He pressed his lips together. "I don't know. My mama is . . . a bull. You know. Stubborn." He laughed a little. "But I will see what I can do. I appreciate your trying. I know how much you care."

Truthfully, Audrey didn't know what she would be able to do with the poor pup. There were so many mystery illnesses out there that never were discovered, and this was probably one of them. She'd already had her look at Bambino, and so had the vets in Palermo. Sometimes, a doctor had to let go and admit that the solution was out of her hands.

"So . . . statement." She took a deep breath and proceeded to say, "I spoke to an orange vendor who mentioned seeing a poacher on the grounds while he was there picking up oranges the day of the murder. I followed his description of the car to Ricardo, the man who runs the rabbit-stand in the market." She pointed in the general direction. "When I asked him about it, he admitted that he had been hunting on those grounds for years. I asked him if he accidentally killed the man who was found dead, there, but he denied doing that. And when the detective came to question him, he made a break for it. So I--"

"Porca miseria!"

Audrey stared at him, trying to understand. Pig . . . misery? She hadn't heard that one before.

Officer Ricci had been quickly scribbling this all down, but in the middle of it, the point on his pencil snapped. He stared at it. "Ah. I don't have another."

"Oh. No problem. I have one." She reached into her tiny bag and saw the vial of blue liquid, taking up much of the real estate inside. She lifted it out and found a ballpoint pen, buried at the bottom of the bag. "Here you go."

"Ah, *grazie,*" he said, taking the pen and grinning as she placed the vial back inside. "I see you got taken by *Signora* Carina, too."

She snapped her bag closed, a little embarrassed. "Uh, well—"

"*Mi mama,* she got the blue liquid, too. For clarity, eh? I don't think it worked. Mama just as confused as always. Especially with Bambino." He shrugged.

Oh, well, she thought. She knew it'd be a waste of twenty euros. But that's how desperate she was. Sometimes people did that, placing their hope in crazy, off-the-wall solutions. Maybe Mrs. Ricci was in a similarly confusing situation and wanted answers, too. She was clearly someone who'd exhaust all avenues to find a solution, judging from how passionate she'd been about getting help for Bambino . . .

Bambino.

Suddenly, the pieces clicked into place. She reached over and locked a hand around the officer's thick forearm, squeezing hard. He stared at her. *"Dottore Smart?* Is everything okay?"

"Officer Ricci . . . you say your mother bought the blue potion? When was that?"

"I don't . . ." He scratched the side of his head with the ballpoint pen. "Last week sometime."

"And did you see her take it?"

He shook his head. "No. But it was gone the next day when I went there. She'd called me over because she told me Bambino was sick."

"Wait . . . so he became sick after she got the potion?"

He nodded. "Why?"

She grabbed his arm. "Can you take me to her house, right away? I need to see Bambino."

"But—"

"Please! I think I know what's wrong with him!" she shouted, running for the police car. This time, Office Ricci followed.

*

Mrs. Ricci's house was not far from the market, closer to the center of town but in the more run-down part of Mussomeli. The moment that the patrol car pulled up in front of the tiny home and Officer Ricci pointed it out, Audrey jumped out and took the stairs two at a time. She knocked feverishly on the door until the woman answered.

"Signora Ricci?" she asked, as the woman stared at her, confused. "It's me, Dr. Smart. I was wondering if I could take a look at Bambino?"

Her eyes flooded with recognition. "Oh! Oh, no! No no!"

"Mama!" Officer Ricci called from behind her. She moved aside as the officer said something to his mother in Italian. Something about how this doctor was good and would never hurt Bambino.

The woman who'd been called a bull by her son showed just how bullish she could be. She planted her feet and shook her head, muttering something about the mafia and murder.

"But I don't associate with the mafia! And the murderer has been found!" Audrey said desperately. There was no time to lose.

Ricci held up a hand and spoke in Italian, explaining that to the old woman. Eventually, the woman sighed. Still giving Audrey the evil eye, she moved aside and pointed into the living area.

Audrey rushed through the tiny kitchen and into a small living space, with a worn sofa and an old-style box television set, on low. The place was full of religious relics, statues of saints and Jesus which all seemed to be staring down, watching over the poor Bambino, who lay curled up on a small dog bed.

She dropped to her knees and checked his pulse. It was very faint. Petting his ears, she looked up at the pair, who had followed her into the living room. "Officer Ricci, can you please ask your mother if Bambino drank some of the potion she bought at the market?"

He nodded and asked her the question. She shook her head.

"No," he said.

She frowned. "No? Are you sure? Because--"

The woman said something, gesturing wildly. Officer Ricci said, "She says she drank it, and it gave her a stomachache."

"But Bambino didn't perhaps have a little? Like, maybe it was left somewhere where the dog could've—"

He'd already started to translate but she cut him off, angrily this time. Audrey could tell that the women felt this was a waste of time. And maybe it was. She'd been so sure. The answer had been perfect. It made absolute sense that the dog had taken the potion with lupine in it and gotten sick. The symptoms were classic.

She straightened, wondering what else to do. "I don't understand. This makes no sense. The lupine in the potion would explain all of Bambino's symptoms, even—"

"*Lupino?*" Mrs. Ricci suddenly exclaimed.

Audrey nodded. "Yes. *Lupino*. It's a flowering plant. And it's toxic to animals. It's long, and it has pink and purple blooms, and—"

"*Lupino!*" The woman said and pulled back the curtain to a back garden. There were several flowering plants, just as Audrey had described. Lupine.

"When were those planted?" Audrey asked.

Officer Ricci said, "She did it a few days ago," Audrey knew she had her answer.

"And has he been outside, eating the plants at all?"

The officer translated, and Mrs. Ricci nodded.

148

Audrey smiled. "That's it. If you keep him away from those plants, he will get better. I can prescribe something to help him feel better until then."

Officer Ricci nodded and translated. Mrs. Ricci beamed and clapped her hands. Then she came over to Audrey, tears in her eyes, and just when Audrey thought she might reach out and smack her, pulled her into a hug. Shocked, Audrey hugged her back.

"It's no problem," she said, tears now in her own eyes. "Really. This is what I do."

Holding Audrey's face between her hands, the old woman kissed both cheeks with gusto.

Officer Ricci laughed. "Can I drive you somewhere, *Dottore?*"

"No, I think I'll walk," she said. "But I'll make sure that prescription gets to you right away so that Bambino's on the mend. And please, if anything else happens, don't hesitate to let me know!"

Ricci walked her to the door. "Don't worry. She'll be a loyal customer for life, now."

"I'm glad."

Audrey went outside, stepped down to the sidewalk, and headed toward the clinic, smiling. The sun was shining brightly, and this time, rather by being annoyed by the heat, she savored it. It felt like a huge weight had just been lifted from her chest, as if now, she knew everything would be okay.

No, she didn't have all the answers. But at least she knew now that she wasn't powerless against finding them.

She thought about something her father had said, long ago, when he had mountains of tasks before him in order to complete a house project. *One thing at a time is all we can do.*

And I will. I'll find the answers. I just can't give up.

But there was one thing that was still bothering her, and as soon as the clinic came into view, she realized what it was. There had been two calls to the clinic after the murder that had brought her out to the Tivoli estate—one from Ricardo, the poacher . . . and the second one, later, someone pretending to be Rafael . . . from whom?

She recalled what Ricardo had said. *I didn't realize until later that anyone had moved in.*

In fact, very few people knew that Rafael lived there. At least, they didn't know him by name. It was the *last* name that seemed to ruffle feathers. People just knew that a Piccolo had moved in. That was all.

And yet, when Concetta had relayed the message, she'd told Audrey that Rafael had called.

Though he'd been very good at keeping to himself, *someone* had known Rafael was there.

She stopped, suddenly, when the answer came to her.

Then she took off in the opposite direction, rushing as fast as she possibly could go.

CHAPTER TWENTY FOUR

This time, when Audrey arrived at the Tivoli estate, she didn't bother to climb the wall and peek in like some devious stalker. She felt far more comfortable than during her previous visits. After all, according to the police, she'd solved the murder that might've otherwise landed in their laps.

But she was a little hesitant when she went around to the front of the house and saw even more dark town cars than before. It looked like an important person's funeral procession.

Don't worry about it, Audrey. They should welcome you with open arms, perhaps even pin a mafia medal on you.

She rang the doorbell. When the door opened, it was Rafael.

"Audrey!" He seemed both pleased and a little frightened to see her there.

"Rafael. Hi . . ." She noticed the tension in his face, the exaggerated lines. Before, she'd have put him at late thirties, but now, he looked much older. "Is everything all right?"

He looked over his shoulder for a moment, then slipped out onto the front porch. "Well, it is kind of a bad time. What brings you here?"

"Did you hear that the murderer has been found?"

His eyes widened. "No. Is it true?"

She nodded. "It was a man who was using the land, poaching animals. He didn't think anyone was on the land. When he shot the man, he panicked, ran off, and called me, hoping I'd find the guy and be able to help him. It was an accident. But he didn't tell the police because he didn't want to get caught trespassing on your land."

"Ah. Really?" He pressed his lips together. "That is good news. But I don't understand. The police worked all this out?"

She shook her head. "Well . . . no. I did."

"*You?*"

She gave him a sheepish shrug. "But I did have another question for you. Something that just doesn't fit. I'm just trying to tie up loose ends and there are a few things that don't make sense."

Behind him, several men were arguing, their voices raised in angry Italian. He looked behind him again. "Well, it's not really a good time . . ."

It certainly didn't feel like one, which was odd. Why would they be worried, if the murderer had been found? Shouldn't they be relaxing. Celebrating? "I promise you. It won't take long. There's one thing in particular I think you might be able to answer."

The arguing inside was reaching a fever pitch, which seemed to distress him greatly. He reached inside and pulled the door closed. "All right. What is it?"

"Well, that second call to the clinic wasn't the poacher, and I really don't see how it could be anyone else in town, since no one knew you by name. It was *you*, wasn't it?"

Now it was his turn to be sheepish. "You are a clever one, aren't you? Yes, it was me. I'd wanted you to come for dinner."

"Why did you lie?"

He let out a distressed little laugh. "I promise you, it had nothing to do with the murder. My cousins were there. They'd just arrived, and I hadn't expected them until the following day. If they knew that I was sweet on a girl, I'd never hear the end of it." He spread out his hands. "I am sorry."

She couldn't help it. She started to laugh. Here was this powerful mafia man, behaving like a high school boy. "I understand," she said, leaning in and winking. "But your secret is safe with me."

"That is nice for you to say. And I hope that when everything is said and done, you will be willing to have dinner with me sometime?"

"Well . . . we'll have to see about that. Truthfully, I'm not sure if I can keep up with your exciting life. Tell me, why do you still seem so upset? I thought you'd be so relieved, celebrating the news. Don't you think the Grinnelli clan will stop the war, once the news gets out that you had nothing to do with it?"

His face turned grave. "No. I don't think so. Some things were put into motion, and I do not think it can be undone. It's too late. War is inevitable."

"What are you talking about?"

He closed his eyes and let out an uneasy breath. "It is terrible, Audrey. They kidnapped my young cousin, Rocco."

Her eyes widened. "What? When?"

152

"Not long. Stupid kid went to town to get breakfast. I told him he needed to lie low, but he never listens to me. We received a text message a few moments ago from his phone. They are in town, and they have him. They will not keep him alive for long."

She clasped a hand over her mouth. "How terrible."

"You know how I wanted peace. But now I think it is too late for that."

"Oh, my gosh," she breathed, her eyes practically popping out of her head. She couldn't believe she was in the middle of this. "But once they find out that you had nothing to do with it—"

"They won't believe it. It is too much of a coincidence. The murder happened on our property. There is no one else that could've done it. They can easily say that we paid the hunter to commit the crime."

"But—"

"Bang!" a high-pitched voice shouted behind her, followed by gleeful, childish laughter.

Audrey whirled around in shock to see a little boy standing there with a toy rifle. He was adorable, no more than eight or nine, and wearing a tiny black suit, a mafia man in training. He was carrying a hunting rifle, a toy version of the one Ricardo had had in his booth. Rafael smiled at him, then shouted, *"Ando, va via!"* He sighed as the kid fiddled with loading the next round. "Kids."

The child scurried off, as suddenly, something came to Audrey. Ugo Telemaco had reporting hearing two shots, in quick succession. A bang-bang, without stop. But if he'd had a hunting rifle like the one that little kid was toting around . . . was that even possible? "So um, I know nothing about guns. With a hunting rifle . . . can you fire off two shots right on top of one another?"

He tilted his head. "No. Not typically. You have to cock or pump the rifle, first, which takes a few seconds."

She stiffened, and suddenly, it came to her. The man that she'd met in town, who was looking for a place to eat. Marco. He was from the mainland, was new to the area. Was he . . . ?

"Oh, my gosh. I think I made a mistake." She backed away. "I have to get back to town. Quick."

A little part of her dreaded the thought of climbing those stairs. It certainly wouldn't be quick, considering how tired she felt. So she was relieved when he fished into the pockets of his slacks and pulled out his keys. "Come on. I'll drive."

CHAPTER TWENTY FIVE

Audrey was right. Rafael Piccolo did know how to travel in style. It was a sporty Mercedes that looked like it'd just been driven out of the showroom.

Not that she had much time to enjoy the ride in the sleek black sportscar with its buttery leather seats, plush interior and every bell and whistle under the sun. Looking up at the sky through the moonroof, she had to wonder—was this the best choice for a man who wanted to be inconspicuous? Perhaps the dark sunglasses he wore, and the tinted windows helped.

She gave him directions to *La Mela Verde,* and they pulled up to the restaurant, minutes later. She hopped out, even before the car had come to a complete stop and rushed inside.

G was there, alone, cleaning up after the lunch rush. His eyes lit up when he saw her. *"Principessa!"* he bellowed. "Can I get you some *ciambotta?"*

"No," she said, out of breath, "But I do need your help. There was a customer here, a couple days ago. He wasn't from here. I think he was Italian, from the mainland. He said his name was Marco. You wouldn't happen to remember him, would you?"

Even as Audrey said it, she knew just how impossible a task it was, like remembering what one had for dinner on this date, a year ago. G saw probably a thousand customers, every day. Many of them were tourists or transplants from somewhere else. And just about everyone spoke Italian. So she expected him to shake his head and say he couldn't help her.

"Si."

"Really?" He had to be pulling her leg.

He opened his mouth to speak but stopped when the door opened, and Rafael walked in. His eyes narrowed as they trailed outside, to the black sportscar on the curb. *"Tu chi sei?"*

"Uh, G," she said, taking Rafael by the sleeve and bringing him forward. "This is Rafael. Rafael, G . . ."

"You're a Piccolo," G said, his voice low and a bit more growly than Audrey had ever heard it.

Rafael nodded. "Nice to meet you, too."

"*Principessa*," he said, his eyes not leaving Rafael's. "Why do you surround yourself with this man? He's from a bad family."

Audrey frowned. "But I thought you told me that it didn't exist here in M—"

"I was wrong. I see that they're back."

The tension was so thick that Audrey probably couldn't have cut it with a steak knife. She said, "All right. Yes. Rafael knows all that. But I think I know who committed that murder in the orange grove. And I need your help."

His eyes finally flickered to Audrey's. "Why are you caught up in this?"

"G, *please*," she begged.

He let out a tired sigh. "All right. How can I help you?"

"That man that was here. Marco. How do you remember him?"

"Because we don't get many from the mainland here. Especially in Mussomeli. They no like us very much here, and we them. But I talk to him. I talk to everyone." He smiled. "He told me he's staying at the Viola. On *via Boccaccio*."

"Really? Oh, perfect! I could just kiss you!" she said, grabbing his hand on the counter and squeezing it. She spun around and headed for the door. Rafael was already holding it open for her. "Thank you!"

"Be careful!" G called after her.

She pulled out her phone and found a listing for the Viola Hotel. Following her GPS, she walked quickly toward the location, with Rafael following close behind.

"What are you thinking, Audrey? Are you saying that the hunter did not kill Pietro, now?"

"Right. I don't think it's possible, and I think the police will realize it, too. He had a hunting rifle. Not a pistol. And there were two shots, one right after another. So, I think it might be someone else."

"Someone else? Who is this Marco?"

"Maybe you can tell me, I hope," she said as they went through the double doors of the hotel and to the reception desk. It was a small hotel, so she hoped that the employees would recognize the man. She said to the clerk, "Hi, I'm looking for a man named Marco. He had a dark beard, glasses, tall and heavyset?"

The woman nodded and checked the registry. "Marco Pollaco, Room 118. Right that way."

"Thank you," Audrey said, stepping away from the desk and following the woman's pointed finger. They walked down a long, paneled hallway, decorated with photographs from around Mussomeli. Rafael got there before her, listened at the door for a moment, and then knocked.

When the door swung open, Marco stood there, his eyes going from Audrey to Rafael.

He didn't seem surprised at all to see either of them there.

In fact, he seemed to have expected it, because he was holding a gun, pointed right at Audrey's chest.

*

"Marco Grinnelli," Rafael said, his voice even and low. "I thought it was you."

Audrey, however, could not understand how anyone could stay so calm. Not while peering down the barrel of a gun. She felt everything inside her rebelling. Her bladder threatened to expel its contents. All it would take was one single squeeze, and she'd be dead. "U-um . . ." She stammered. "Grinnelli?"

Marco poked his head out the door, looked up and down the hallway, then grabbed her arm. "Get in here. The both of you. No stupid moves."

She let him pull her inside, and Rafael followed, his hands up, appeasing the man. Though he was complying, Rafael didn't look worried in the least. In fact, he seemed calm, relaxed. Audrey, on the other hand, was sweating, her knees knocking together as she scurried into the room, bumping into the door and other furniture because she refused to take her eyes off the barrel of the gun.

He motioned Rafael forward, while she moved backwards. "Gun," Marco snarled. "Give it to me."

Rafael reached under his blazer and pulled out a pistol, dropping the butt of it into Marco's waiting hand. The backs of her knees hit a bed and she sat down in a rush, just as Rafael exclaimed, "Rocco!"

At that, Audrey tore her eyes from the gun and followed his line of sight to the other bed. Rocco was lying there, tied up, mouth gagged. He, too, looked strangely complacent, as if he'd had this happen to him

157

often. In fact, though his wrists were secured tightly behind his back, he managed to wave a couple fingers.

"How're you doing, boy?"

He somehow shrugged his shoulders.

Rafael shook his head. "What is the meaning of this, Marco? You killed Pietro?"

Marco motioned him to the bed with the gun. "You don't run this, Rafael. I do."

Rafael shrugged and sat down next to Audrey. "All right. Now, what?"

He scowled. "Yeah. I killed Pietro. I was in the orange grove, coming to kill you, but then I saw him there, and I thought he might've been there to rat me out. Pietro was always such a goody-goody, like you, Rafael. And I said, you know what? That'll be better. Start a turf war and give us a chance to blow the Piccolo clan off the map for good. One stone, and a heck of a lot of birds."

Rafael crossed his arms. "For what reason, Marco? We've been living here in Sicily in peace for over twenty years. We have had no beef with you and your clan."

"Yeah, in peace. That's a joke." He shook his head sourly. "You've had rule over the land here for a long time and have done nothing with it. It's time the Grinnellis move in and show how things are really done. We've always known our empire could be huge if we just got our chance to run Sicily. But we couldn't do that, with Piccolos still here, blocking our way."

"You can't do that now," Rafael said. "In case you didn't realize, someone else was arrested for the murder. It wasn't pinned on us."

"I know," he hissed, eyes narrowed on Audrey. "Because of *her*. I was there. I saw the whole thing go down. And that's when I saw Rocco, here. I grabbed him. I figured if he ended up dead, you guys would have to retaliate. Right?"

Rafael nodded, as if it all made sense. "But now you have me and Audrey. So what are you going to do? Are you going to kill us all?"

"That's right. More bang for my buck." He grinned wickedly.

Audrey shuddered. He said it far too nonchalantly for her liking, like someone who'd murdered many times before. Of course, he was the killer. He was right out of a movie. A heartless mafioso, just like Luigi had warned her about. This was what he'd told her to stay away from.

158

And so it only made sense that she was here, now, with a pistol pointed straight at her heart.

"You can't shoot us here. Someone's going to hear, you know," she squeaked.

He looked around. "I know, but that's no problem. I've got it all figured out. You three, and me, are going to take a little ride to the orange groves." He lifted the phone in his hands and looked at Rafael. "You, take your car out to the back and text your cousin's line when you get there. And no funny business. If I don't get that text in one minute, your girlfriend here is dead."

He grabbed her and pulled her up. Audrey gasped in horror as she felt the gun, digging into her ribs. Before then, she'd almost convinced herself that this was all a bad nightmare she'd soon wake up from. But feeling the pressure of the gun against her side made it all real. "Rafael!" she whimpered.

He reached into his pocket, pulled out his keys, and held up his hands to calm her down. "Do not worry, *cara*. I will not let anything happen to you."

And then he went out the door, leaving Audrey there with the two strange mafia men, and her heart in her throat.

*

"Just drive," Marco said from the passenger seat, gun pointed right at Rafael's side.

"This is foolish," Rafael said as they left the town limits of Mussomeli, headed downhill, toward the orange grove. "Folly. We Piccolos want peace. Most of the Grinnelli clan does, too. But you want to engage in a war so that you and the Grinnellis can take over this land and expand an already dying empire? It's foolish."

Marco donned his dark sunglasses and stared out the window, letting the wind blow back his dark hair. "I said, just drive. No commentary." He shook his head. "You and Pietro were that new breed of family, who want to play things straight. But that's foolish. You never get ahead, playing by the rules. And when I get you three out there, and you're each found with bullets to the brain, your mafia family will have no choice to come after us. And we'll destroy them. We're bigger, and more prepared. And we'll decimate you, leaving all of Sicily to be ours to claim."

Rafael shook his head. "You want Sicily? Take it. Take it all from us. The killing stops here."

Marco snorted. "Where have I heard that before? Oh, right. Right before your father killed my father."

Audrey's eyes widened. "Is that true?"

Next to her, Rocco, still bound and gagged, nodded, still looking rather calm. Audrey shifted uncomfortably in her seat, feeling like she was on her way to her own funeral. She felt like she should say something, but at the same time, she was sure it wouldn't matter. There were decades of bad blood between the Piccolos and the Grinnellis. She had a feeling that even if she sat with them for hours, she'd never be able to disentangle the sordid history that bound these two families together. It was probably a worse saga than the Capulets and Montagues.

And it had nothing to do with her. But yet, once again, here she was, in the middle of it. Wrong place, wrong time.

She watched with dread as the street became narrower and the first of the orange trees came into view. Marco motioned for him to pull into a dirt access driveway that ran along the edge of the grove, separating the Tivoli estate from the property that belonged to Ugo Telemaco. The Mercedes bumped onto the rutted drive, past the stone wall, and headed through the thick tangle of orange trees. Their leaves blocked out the setting sun, casting them in a nightlike darkness.

Audrey shuddered as Marco directed him to stop the car. Rafael did as he was told, slowly braking and then cutting the engine. "What do you want from us, now?"

Marco motioned with the gun. "What do you think? Out of the car. Now. Move it."

Audrey opened the door, feeling faint. Since Rocco was tied up, when he shuffled toward her, she helped him out and closed the door. Rafael went over to her, and for the first time, he looked guilty. His expression said, *I'm sorry I got you into this.*

At that moment, she really didn't care how she'd gotten into it. Now, she was looking around, trying to determine how to get out of it. And it seemed pretty hopeless. The mansion for the Tivoli estate was probably a mile away from where they stood, on the outskirts of the grove. There was no chance that Rafael's men back at the house could've heard their car, pulling up. And without them, what could the three of them do? What chance did three unarmed people have against a hardened mafia man and his gun?

"Stand here. Line up. Turn around. Come on. I don't got all day."

"Marco," Rafael said evenly. "This is your last chance. You don't have to do this."

He laughed bitterly. "For the last time, Piccolo. *Turn. Around.*"

Even at that moment, she couldn't fully believe that this was happening to her. It'd all seemed so outrageous, like a joke. But right then, the full weight of what was going on hit her. She turned around, hands lifted in surrender, looking up at the trees. They were moving, but it was a windy day. Were they just swaying in the wind? Was there no one around? No hope at all of rescue at all?

Rafael came shoulder to shoulder with her and murmured, "I'm sorry, *cara*. I didn't mean for things to end this way."

She nearly choked on her breath. For things to end this way? Was this the end? Her stomach, which had already felt queasy, now dropped completely. He'd promised her she'd be all right, and now, was he going back on it? She bit her tongue so hard that she tasted blood. Was the next thing she felt going to be a bullet in her back? There was the unmistakable crack of him cocking his gun. She gritted her teeth and closed her eyes, and . . .

Suddenly a big gust of wind whistled through the trees and there was the thundering sound of footsteps on the hard ground. She looked up just as a number of men in suits burst through the line of trees, guns drawn. At the head of them was Giuseppe. "Drop it, Marco. Now."

Marco cursed under his breath. Audrey turned to see him scanning the area. They were surrounded by at least thirty men in suits, what had to have been the entire Piccolo clan. Every one of them was pointing a gun at Marco.

For a moment, Audrey was sure he'd come out shooting. His face was red with anger and his scowl was that of pure hatred. "You all can go to—"

"*Marco*," Giuseppe barked, scolding him like a child. "You know you're outnumbered. Don't let us kill you. It's time to go home and end this. For good."

Marco's eyes went wide, and his face crumpled. He dropped his gun, then got to his knees. His shoulders sagged. Suddenly, the once frightening mafioso put his hands to his face and began to sob. Giuseppe sighed and lowered his gun. "There's a good lad, Marco.

Come on," he said in a very grandfatherly voice, motioning for the other men to drop their guns, which they did without question. "We'll get you inside, get you some minestrone, and send you back to Italia. To your family. And we can put all this behind us. Okay?"

He nodded through his sobs and allowed Giuseppe to lift him up and walk him toward the house. Audrey stared as they walked him away. "What just happened here?" she whispered to Rafael.

He shrugged. "Marco's always been the unbalanced one in the Grinnelli family. A troublemaker. I thought he'd gone away from his family, but I see he hasn't. It does not surprise me in the least that he wanted to start this war."

"I can't believe it," she said as the two men disappeared into the grove, followed by the other Piccolo family members. "I don't think he's going to be able to go back to Italy, just like that. The police will be coming after him."

"Oh, they will, don't worry. We will call them, once the Don has had his chance to deal with him."

She raised an eyebrow. "You will? Because I had poor Ricardo, the poacher, arrested for—"

He nodded. "Don't worry about that. We'll clear it up. But I think it's probably a good thing that Ricardo stays in hot water for now, considering he was hunting illegally on my land. Don't you think so?"

"I suppose so. And how did your men know that we were going to be—"

He laughed. "I'm not an idiot, Audrey. But apparently, *Marco* is. I texted them when he sent me to bring the car around back."

"Oh." That made absolute sense. "I guess I didn't even think about that. I was too busy freaking out over the gun pointed at my face. I'm so glad at least one of us kept a clear head during things like that, because I couldn't think. Something tells me you've been in situations like that before."

He shrugged. "Once or twice." He held out his bent arm to her. "Now that that business is taken care of, how would you like to join me and the boys for a nice bowl of minestrone? Did he tell you, Giuseppe makes the best minestrone on the whole planet?"

She smiled. "Well, I—"

"It's the least we can do to thank you. You prevented a big war between our families. We're very grateful."

"In that case, I don't mind if I do." She slipped her hand into his offered arm, and together, they walked back to the Tivoli mansion.

CHAPTER TWENTY SIX

That evening, in the gorgeous courtyard, lit with fairy lights, the members of the Piccolo clan sat around a massive, long table, where there was plenty of minestrone and red wine to go around. Giuseppe sat at one end, with Audrey catty-corner to him, and Rafael on her other side. The head chair on the other side of the table was, oddly, empty. The chatter was mostly Italian, very little of which Audrey understood, but she couldn't deny that everyone was in a good mood, and it made her smile, too.

As they waited for the first course, Marta came out and whispered in Rafael's ear. He nodded, wiped his mouth on a napkin, and stood up. "One moment," he said, smiling at Audrey.

When he was gone, Giuseppe leaned in and said, "So you did not take my advice about staying out of things."

She gritted her teeth and gave him a sheepish look. "I'm sorry. I tried to. But I guess my curiosity keeps getting in the way."

"It's all right. I suppose it makes sense, you being a doctor and all. You're never satisfied until you have all the answers," he said, winking at her.

A moment later, the door to the house swung open, and three men appeared. One was Rafael, and on the other end was Marco, head town, tail firmly between his legs. They were escorting a hunched man with a cane. He was frail, with pure white hair, abundant wrinkles and had to have been at least ninety years old. Rafael slowly led him to the chair at the other side of the table, and as he sat down, everyone seemed to bow their heads in reverence.

Giuseppe leaned in. "Don Piccolo," he said in a low voice. "He has been our leader for over forty years."

"Oh . . ." Audrey breathed.

Marco took the seat beside him. After settling them both in and pouring their wine, Rafael jogged over to his seat and sat down across from Audrey. He nodded and said, "My grandfather."

Audrey nodded. "But why is Marco—"

"It's tradition. We share meals with our enemies. If you're willing to eat with those who will betray you, it shows that you are the bigger man," he whispered to her.

"But the police—"

"They're on their way. Our business with him is done. He'll be handed over to them for whatever justice they feel fit to pursue," he explained.

The old man at the end of the table rose to his feet and lifted his glass. He spoke in Italian for a while, in such a soft voice that Audrey zoned out. She couldn't believe she was here, sharing a meal with a mafia family. "Audrey Smart?"

The mention of her name jolted her back to reality. She blinked to see Don Piccolo, staring at her. "To Audrey Smart!" he said in very broken English. "Who saved our people from a bloody war. The Piccolo *familia* is forever grateful. *Salud!*"

The room erupted into cheers and everyone drank.

Audrey blushed as she beamed. "Thank you," she whispered. "It was nothing."

Rafael leaned over to us. "It was not nothing. In fact, it was very important to us. You will always have a place at our table, and we will always have your back. In fact, a favor like this must be repaid. If there is anything you desire, any favor I can do for you, please, let me know."

She blinked. "A favor?"

"That's right."

She thought about the silly potion she'd purchased to give her clarity, and of the wishes she'd had for finding out which man to pursue. She doubted Rafael could help with that—in fact, he seemed to only be complicating it, not that she would ever willingly date a mafia man. She'd had far too much excitement over the past two days to know that she didn't like living life in that kind of fast lane.

Then, she thought of the clinic. Two months ago, she'd have loved to ask for the men's brawn to help her fix the place up. But she'd made great strides with the clinic, and now she had Concetta to help. So she really didn't need a favor where that was concerned, either.

Next, she thought about her house. While Audrey always complained about all the work and often envied Nessa for having scores of men to help with her renovation, she wasn't sure she wanted a bunch of mafia people helping her with those tasks. Actually, she liked handling most of the stuff herself. Her father had always said that doing something on one's own was the best way to feel pride of workmanship. And he was right. That was another reason why she hadn't constantly been calling Mason over for help. She wanted it to be *her* home. *Her* work. *Her* blood, sweat, and tears. *Her* pride and joy.

So the only thing that left was . . . of course.

"Would you be able to find someone for me?" she blurted suddenly, as Marta set a steaming bowl of red soup in front of her. It smelled delicious, but Audrey was now caught up by the excitement of this potential favor.

Rafael smiled. "You intrigue me. Who is this someone?"

"My father," she said softly. "But he's been missing for over twenty years. The last I heard, he was in Montagna, but that was years ago. I don't know if he'd even want to talk to me, but I do wonder where he is, and what he's doing now. He's my dad."

She'd gone and gotten a little teary-eyed, at the thought of him, her voice faraway and weak. She recovered quickly and shrugged.

Rafael and Giuseppe looked at each other and nodded. Rafael said, "I do have some experience with that. I have resources I might be able to tap, to help you."

"That would be absolutely amazing," she said, dipping her spoon into the soup and taking a taste. "And wow. You are right, Rafael. This has to be the best minestrone on the planet!"

*

Four days later, Audrey buckled down and finished repairing the pits on the remaining three walls in the living area. It required waking up at four in the morning for the past two days, working until her fingers ached, but when she repaired the last divot, she stretched her hands over her head in her oversized denim overalls to release the sore muscles in her lower back, and smiled. *Things are definitely coming along.*

"Looks good, right Bub?" she asked Nick, who was busy chewing on a dog toy she'd given to him as a treat for helping catch Ricardo. Even though Ricardo hadn't been the killer, Nick had gone above and beyond the call of duty.

However, as much as he cared to defend her, he really didn't seem to care much about the state of the walls in the living room. She sighed. "You're a tough customer to impress."

Someone knocked on the door. "Mail call!" a voice shouted outside.

She grinned as she stared up at the perfectly smooth wall. Everything had been such a mess before, but just like her dad had told her, things were coming together, one by one. For the first time in a long while, she felt relaxed. Content. And maybe she didn't have all the answers about the men in her life, but she felt like eventually, they'd come, just like the other ones had.

She called, "In here, Mace!"

A second later, he appeared in the doorway, holding a pile of her mail. He looked around, inspecting her handiwork as Nick rushed up to him for a pet. "Looking good. Anyone ever tell you thatyou might have a future in plaster? Couldn't have done it better, myself, Boston."

"I know, turns out, I don't need you for much," she said, using some of the ego he was so fond of throwing at her.

"How about the faucet?"

"Oh! I fixed it myself," she said with another casual shrug, even though the solution to that had been anything but easy. She'd spent a good three hours trying to get the right washer to fit in the right place, and finally stop the leak. It'd taken a couple of days, but the first floor of her house had finally dried out.

"I am shocked."

So was she, actually. But as much as she appreciated help from others, she loved figuring things out herself. That was the reason she'd become a vet in the first place—she loved solving these little mysteries—whether it be in a little puppy, a broken faucet, or a murder in an orange grove.

"I'm going to head to the hardware store to pick out paint colors tonight, I think."

"What color are you thinking of?"

"Blue," she said immediately. "A pale, sky blue. What do you think?"

He inspected it closer. "Blue works." He set her mail down on the top step. "So I heard the case of the murdered mafia guy was solved, huh? Did you have anything to do with that?"

"Me?" she said innocently. She thought about telling him of all the excitement with Ricardo and Marco and being held at gunpoint, so close to death, but decided not to. He was always telling her she needed to be more careful, and she didn't need another lecture. "Why would you even think that from little ol' me?"

He snickered. "I don't know. Just a hunch. Because little ol' you is a pain in the rump. The last time I saw you, you were kind of frantic, freaking out about how you found the body. Then you had that other guy show up on your doorstep. And, also, because you had a hand in finding all the other killers around here."

"Oh." Well, he was right about that. "But the truth is, I don't think I want to associate with mafia. It's not a good look for me. Business at the clinic took a big nosedive—half of the people thought I was a murderer, and half of them thought I was married to the mob. It's finally coming back, thank goodness. I have a full day of appointments tomorrow. But I think I need to stay away from organized crime."

He raised an eyebrow and smirked. "Even good-looking, charming mafia guys who show up at your place, bearing citrus?"

Her mouth opened. She'd forgotten he'd seen Rafael at her home, and Mason had seemed a little upset, then. Which was ridiculous. He had no reason to be. She and Rafael would never be more than just friends. "I'm sorry. Am I sensing jealousy?"

He shrugged. "Nothing to sense. I'm just making an observation. He was charming and he brought you fruit, and his face didn't look too much like it'd been chewed up and spit out."

She grinned at him. "You're good-looking, charming, and bring me pie. I think you win." When he laughed, she added, "And, I'm not so stupid as to date a guy who comes from a family of killers. In fact, like I said, from now on, I'm keeping my distance."

He eyed her skeptically. "That's the thing about organized crime. They call you, you'd better come, or hell hath no fury. You'll be ruing the day you said no."

She laughed and picked up Nick, stroking his fur. He took his pets and jumped quickly off her leg, disappearing out the window, a regular ninja. "Don't be silly. They won't call me! Rafael doesn't have any pets, so he has no need for help from me."

"You're serious?"

She nodded. "Yes. No more trouble for me. I've had enough to last me a lifetime. And by the way, I don't even like oranges, so help yourself."

He glanced into the kitchen, at the huge basket of them, which had been relatively untouched since she received it. Nick had made a dent in them, but it was still a mountain that took up most of the little bistro table in the kitchen. "Maybe I will. But not right now. I need something more. Want to go out for a bite?"

She wiped the trowel on her pant leg and gnawed on her lip, averting his eyes by staring up at the wall. She knew that if she took one look into those blue eyes, she'd probably cave like a house of cards. And she'd decided not to get into this. Not now. Not until she was sure what she wanted and that no one would get hurt. "Well, I still have to clean all this mess up, and—"

"You did say you wanted to take a raincheck after your poor showing during our last date . . . remember?" He crossed his arms and leaned casually against the wall. "'Cause I remember. I remember slaving all day to make you fried chicken and having you spend the whole time yawning and telling me you wanted to go home."

She winced. "All day?"

"Well. Maybe not all day. But close."

She sighed. "I'm sorry. I know, we do need to re-do that date, but I'm—" She looked down at her dirty overalls. Her hair was in a messy bun. But it wasn't just that. She still hadn't made much of a decision regarding G. So she shrugged. "Look at me. I look terrible."

"You look pretty hot. I love overalls on chicks. It's like my top fantasy," he said with a grin. When she gave him a horrified look, he added, "Come on. It's not a date, if you're all worried about that. Just dinner. I didn't eat either and I'm so hungry my stomach's done think my throat's been cut."

She smiled at his little Southernism, then pulled her hair out of the tie, and scraped it together again. "All right, all right. Maybe we can stop by the hardware store, too, and you can help me pick out the blue?"

"You got it."

As she went down the stairs to the kitchen, she scooped up the mail. Most of it was advertisements, postcards for new businesses in the area run by other expats who'd recently moved to the area. But as she leafed through them, discarding the junk mail in the trash, she came upon a large envelope, made of thick, creamy stock. It looked like the type of paper one would use for a wedding invitation, back in the States. There was no return address, but it was made out to a *Dottore Audrey Smart*.

She stared at it for a moment before sliding a finger under the flap and pulling out a piece of stiff cardstock. It was in Italian, but she translated as best she could:

You are cordially invited to a dinner party to be given by the Family Piccolo . . .

She stared at it so long, her retinas burned. Mason was clearly worried, because he said, "What? What is it? Are you okay?" He peered over her shoulder to catch sight of it and whistled. "Woo-wee. I'd say someone's about to get her corn creamed."

She had no clue what it meant to have one's corn creamed, but her insides did feel like that—mushy and sick. Her appetite rushed away. A family gathering with the Piccolos? It sounded like the beginning of trouble.

And so much for staying out of the way of that.

NOW AVAILABLE!

A VILLA IN SICILY: CANNOLI AND A CASUALTY
(A Cats and Dogs Cozy Mystery—Book 6)

"Very entertaining. Highly recommended for the permanent library of any reader who appreciates a well-written mystery with twists and an intelligent plot. You will not be disappointed. Excellent way to spend a cold weekend!"
--Books and Movie Reviews (regarding *Murder in the Manor*)

A VILLA IN SICILY: CANNOLI AND A CASUALTY is book #6 in a charming new cozy mystery series by bestselling author Fiona Grace, author of *Murder in the Manor*, a #1 Bestseller with over 100 five-star reviews (and a free download)!

Audrey Smart, 34, has made a major life change, walking away from her life as a vet (and from a string of failed romances) and moving to Sicily to buy a $1 home—and embark on a mandatory renovation she knows nothing about. She finds herself busy running the town's new shelter, while also renovating her own problematic home—and dating again.

Audrey's love life is heating up, and when his prominent Sicilian family invites Audrey to a family feast in Palermo, it's an offer she can't refuse. It's everything she needs: new friends, a huge, new family, and food to die for.

But *la dolce vita* isn't what it seems. When Audrey overhears word of a looming mafia vengeance hit, the only person pleading for the life of the innocent target is her. With just a few days to prove they have the wrong man, can Audrey assuage their anger and discover who really killed the mafiosi?

Finding herself in the middle of two rival mafia families, Audrey can't help but wonder: is she in way over her head?

A laugh-out-loud cozy packed with mystery, intrigue, renovation, animals, food, wine—and of course, love—A VILLA IN SICILY will capture your heart and keep you glued to the very last page.

More books in the series will be available soon!

Fiona Grace

Fiona Grace is author of the LACEY DOYLE COZY MYSTERY series, comprising nine books; of the TUSCAN VINEYARD COZY MYSTERY series, comprising seven books; of the DUBIOUS WITCH COZY MYSTERY series, comprising three books; of the BEACHFRONT BAKERY COZY MYSTERY series, comprising six books; and of the CATS AND DOGS COZY MYSTERY series, comprising nine books.

Fiona would love to hear from you, so please visit www.fionagraceauthor.com to receive free ebooks, hear the latest news, and stay in touch.

BOOKS BY FIONA GRACE

LACEY DOYLE COZY MYSTERY
MURDER IN THE MANOR (Book#1)
DEATH AND A DOG (Book #2)
CRIME IN THE CAFE (Book #3)
VEXED ON A VISIT (Book #4)
KILLED WITH A KISS (Book #5)
PERISHED BY A PAINTING (Book #6)
SILENCED BY A SPELL (Book #7)
FRAMED BY A FORGERY (Book #8)
CATASTROPHE IN A CLOISTER (Book #9)

TUSCAN VINEYARD COZY MYSTERY
AGED FOR MURDER (Book #1)
AGED FOR DEATH (Book #2)
AGED FOR MAYHEM (Book #3)
AGED FOR SEDUCTION (Book #4)
AGED FOR VENGEANCE (Book #5)
AGED FOR ACRIMONY (Book #6)
AGED FOR MALICE (Book #7)

DUBIOUS WITCH COZY MYSTERY
SKEPTIC IN SALEM: AN EPISODE OF MURDER (Book #1)
SKEPTIC IN SALEM: AN EPISODE OF CRIME (Book #2)
SKEPTIC IN SALEM: AN EPISODE OF DEATH (Book #3)

BEACHFRONT BAKERY COZY MYSTERY
BEACHFRONT BAKERY: A KILLER CUPCAKE (Book #1)
BEACHFRONT BAKERY: A MURDEROUS MACARON (Book #2)
BEACHFRONT BAKERY: A PERILOUS CAKE POP (Book #3)
BEACHFRONT BAKERY: A DEADLY DANISH (Book #4)
BEACHFRONT BAKERY: A TREACHEROUS TART (Book #5)
BEACHFRONT BAKERY: A CALAMITOUS COOKIE (Book #6)

CATS AND DOGS COZY MYSTERY
A VILLA IN SICILY: OLIVE OIL AND MURDER (Book #1)
A VILLA IN SICILY: FIGS AND A CADAVER (Book #2)
A VILLA IN SICILY: VINO AND DEATH (Book #3)

Made in the USA
Las Vegas, NV
14 July 2021